My Funny

Major

Medical

Edited By

Linton Robinson

Karla Telega

Bäuu Press
My Funny Books

Published in the USA by
Bäuu Press and My Funny Books

Bäuu Press
P.O. Box 1945
Winter Park, CO 80482
www.bauuinstitute.com

My Funny Books
www.myfunnybooks.biz

CONTENTS

Bedside Miss-Manners
Karla Telega

Have you ever noticed how the usual response from the surgical staff when you wake up during a "procedure" is to stroke your head and say, "It's all right." Seems pretty lame when you're lying there with half a silverware drawer sticking out of your neck. I know, I know. You're all saying, "I hate when that happens!"

At least when I started swatting at the oxygen mask and yelling, "Get it off me! I can't breathe!" they were kind enough to remove the mask and just hold it over my face … as they cranked the anesthesia to Chernobyl. I think I managed to say "Thank you" before slipping into a coma. I'm all about the good manners.

As a society, without proper etiquette, we are little better than rutting warthogs. I've dated a few of them, so I know whereof I speak. I have been in the delicate and vulnerable position of being a hospital patient many times, and would like to address a few "issues" I've had with staff:

- When it is fifty-cent beer night in the recovery room, you might want to offer a pint to the patient. I couldn't believe the nerve of the nurses who were walking around with glasses of beer and not sharing. Had I been a little more lucid, I would have realized that a) there was a big herkin' tube sticking north into one of my southerly orifices, and b) the "keg" was hanging on the side of my bed.

- I'm all for having a little privacy when forced to use a bedpan, but this is not a good time for the nurse to do her nails, have a tryst in the linen closet, or go home. It took four days for the pan imprint to fade from my butt.

- When a patient is hyperventilating, it is best not to administer medication. To her credit, I would like to commend the nurse for her timely execution of the Heimlich maneuver to clear the golf ball size pill from my airway and send it rocketing across the room like a pharmaceutical missile. Her aim was impeccable, as it scored a direct hit on my husband's manhood while he was suggesting that I breathe normally.

- After delivery, is it really necessary to stick the patient in a room next to "the screamer"? I already did my part and pooped a watermelon out of a space which normally accommodates a tampon. I'd prefer not having to listen to the next act warming up.

I understand that there is very little time to observe the niceties when dealing with a gaping chest wound, and I would like to give a shout-out to the emergency room staff at North Arundel Hospital for saving my daughter's life. You all are doing a wonderful job … just watch that bedpan thing. You don't want an oval imprint on your hiney when it's hanging out of a hospital gown.

Previews of Coming Contractions
By Lisa Tognola

Home delivery used to mean a mustached man named Raul driving an oxidized Ford Pinto and tossing the morning newspaper into our neighbor's bushes. That was until my impatient baby made a quick exit onto my living room floor and redefined the term.

It was 12:15 a.m. when I was jolted from my slumber by a drive to my gut with a #5 iron, followed by a series of wrenching contractions at five-minute intervals. This little baby meant business. I felt as anxious as the day I found out I was pregnant with our first child. While my fellow graduate students awaited the results from their Experimental Psychology finals, I sweated out the results of my pregnancy exam at the student health clinic; the brightly colored condoms piled high on the counter, mocking me.

"Honey, wake up—it's happening! I think I'm in full swing!" I yelled to my husband, Chris, who lay as dormant as a bear in hibernation. I repeated myself, and gave him a nudge. He turned over and grumbled, "Keep your eye on the ball!" pulled up the covers and rolled back over. Fighting rapid-fire contractions, I said, "Honey, I think I'm having the baby."

"Baby! Did you say baby?" He did a front round off and vaulted off the bed like an Olympic gymnast.

"Start the car and call Mrs. D," I cried.

I tried to convince myself that this was a false labor, like the kind I once experienced when Chris and I abandoned a rack of lamb and carrots Vichy during a candlelight anniversary dinner at a five-star restaurant and headed straight to the hospital, only to return home to a reheated bowl of yesterday's chili over the 11:00 news.

3

Maybe I was using avoidance due to the stressful conditions of my first birth, which took place at the end of the hallway in an overcrowded hospital bulging with women in labor, something to do with a full moon and the Macy's Annual Sale.

But when embryonic fluid suddenly gushed out of me, I knew there was no denying it. This labor was real. In a panic, I waddled down the stairs and headed to the front stoop, where I collided with Mrs. D, our neighbor. "Where do you think you're going in this snowstorm? You get yourself right back into that house, young lady, or you'll have yourself a car delivery!"

"Yes, Mrs. D," I replied.

Did she say car delivery? In my book the only acceptable car delivery was a newly purchased Baby Benz arriving at my doorstep. Yet I was terrified by the idea of having the baby at home. I let Mrs. D guide me back into the house. Uncertain as to how to proceed, I did what came naturally to me during times of stress. I reached for the cookie jar, and groped my way to the bottom where I located one lone fortune cookie. I cracked it open. "Car delivery today mean messy carpool tomorrow." I imagined what the morning routine might look like.

"Time for school, kids. Get in the car."

"But Mom, there's a giant jellyfish on the floor!"

"Sweety, that sea creature is just mommy's placenta. Now step over the damn thing or we'll be late for school!"

I let Mrs. D guide me back into the house. By now, a team of Brazilian Jiu-Jitsu warriors were trying to fight their way out of my belly and I was beginning to think of childbirth less as a miracle and more as cruel and unusual punishment. I leaned forward, struck my best werewolf pose and let out a primal howl that rivaled the wild dogs in Kujo. Then I dropped down on all fours with my knees cushioned by our new living room carpet—the one that had led us on a three-year quest for the perfect color rug to match our gold and mauve living room.

A generally kind and gentle person, I ordinarily would have welcomed Mrs. D's outreach of affection. But possessed with unworldly pain and glowing red eyes, I hissed, "Get your hands off me!" Mrs. D's arm recoiled from my flaming body. Mrs. D. may have wondered whether she needed to get help, or garnish herself with a string of garlic.

This was not the delivery we had planned. Where was the soothing music, the relaxation mantras, and the blast of narcotics that would send my uterus into a blissful coma? "I don't want to have the baby at home!" I wailed. Nothing changed. A moment later, something changed: I felt the baby's head, and screamed, "I'm having the baby at home!"

Chris assured me, "Everything's going to be okay. Let me give you a hug." Or maybe it was, "Everything's going to be okay, just don't soil the rug." As two policemen stormed through the door, followed by two volunteer emergency medical technicians, I regained hope. But I worried when the EMT's appeared to be younger than my high school babysitter. I wondered whether they'd ever seen a vagina . . .

Within minutes of screaming, "Get this baby out of me!" the baby glided out like a slippery bar of soap into the cradled hands of the EMT. I heard, "It's a boy!"

In overwhelmed relief, I responded, "Towels!"

Chris repeated, "Towels for the baby!" like a short order cook.

"Towels for the rug!" I added. Then I provided detailed instructions on emergency carpet care.

As a group of men stood around my tethered baby scratching their heads, debating how to tie off the umbilical cord without a clamp, I watched Chris reach down to remove his shoelace. I reminded him of the recycling twine in the drawer next to the stove.

After arriving at the hospital, I was finally able to call my parents and congratulate them on the birth of their new grandson while Chris proudly handed out cigars to the staff. Then the nurse called him over to the examining room. A few minutes later, Chris approached. "Lisa, you're not going to be believe this. We don't have a baby boy. It's a girl." I dropped the phone. "The nurse said she looks beautiful. I peeked under the blanket, and she's right, it's a girl," he said, as he tenderly wiped a string of drool from my gaping mouth.

"Lisa, Lisa? Are you there?" I heard my mother's voice from the dangling receiver. I picked up the phone.

"Mom, scratch that. It turns out you have a granddaughter."

"Lisa, did they give you drugs at the hospital?" She asked, trying to rationalize my gender confusion over my own child.

"No mom," I said as I spoke my thoughts out loud. "The baby must have been swollen when she was born and someone thought she was a boy."

"So what they saw wasn't a, a …" my mother asked tentatively.

"Nnnno." With that, I hung up the phone.

The next day, as my husband tried to convince me that it was the EMT and not him who had called out our baby's mistaken gender in all the hullabaloo, the familiar sound of a dragging tail pipe prompted my husband to retrieve the newspaper. This time, Raul's home delivery brought news of my home delivery. The local headline read, "New Baby Boy Girl Born at Home."

THE RUNNING OF THE NOSES

Why I Hate Straws
Barry Parham

That was the day, some 15-plus years ago now, that I personally validated several of our very fine natural laws, mostly Isaac Newton's.

Memorial Day. Lake Secession, South Carolina. A blithely boisterous bonding of friends, food and frolic, punctuated by pork barbecue, parasailing, skiing, sunbathing, and volleyball.

It being yet another thing I'd never tried, I decided to give parasailing a go. My friends gave me the quick "how-to" primer. We laid out the big sail on the grass. I strapped myself in to the harness. The boat accelerated away from the shore. The towline went taut.

And then something went wrong. "Come To Jamaica" ads notwithstanding, I did not rise into the skies. Perhaps as some sort of karmic punishment for voting Republican, I skewed off to the right. I caromed off a large boulder, my body filed a curt complaint with the Lake Secession provisional parliament, and then all these tiny little breath soldiers seceded from my chest nation.

I don't remember passing out, but I do remember floating stupidly in the shallow part of the lake, wondering why I couldn't stand up. I made a couple half-hearted gestures at my friends on the shore, uttered a few Ozzy Osbourne-like quotes, and was shortly hauled out of the lake, just ahead of my new four-piece pelvis.

The trip to the hospital was uneventful, if you define uneventful as "some oddly-bent wet guy cursing at potholes for a half-hour or so." At the hospital, they carefully got me into a nice bed and into a nice semi-coma. For the next week, my constant companion was a little

Pain Management Device, modulated at my whim by a small dial. And I whimmed a lot. By the second day, they had to replace the dial. I don't recall the name of the drug, Nokairzital maybe, but if your hips are ever sub-divided into four smaller hip apartments, I highly recommend it.

For a while, I couldn't even stand, much less walk, canter, trot, lope, kneel, sit, or limbo. And since I couldn't get out of bed, to perform even the most basic personal duties, my medical team called for something called a catheter, which is Latin for "Nurse, you have lost your damn mind. You're gonna put that WHERE?"

I tried to talk them out of it. I mean, I really, really tried. No innocent man, mistakenly hauled into court, ever mounted such a defense. I suggested they had misread the Nurses Manual, or had not really been paying attention in medical school on Catheter Day. But despite all my frantically scribbled mechanical drawings, they insisted. So I reached for my little Pain Management Device, spun the dial up to "Woodstock" and lapsed into a discomforted drowse. And then…well…other things happened.

To this day, whenever I see a straw, I have hateful, violent, anti-social thoughts.

And then came the day of reckoning.

"Okay, Mr. Parham. Today, we're gonna remove the catheter. But if you can't take care of business, we'll have to put it back. Okay?"

In a life full of challenges, diversions and wonders, I have often found myself needing to focus my concentration. Let's just say that, on that day, I took concentration to a whole new level. I didn't just successfully command my kidneys – I think I levitated the cafeteria.

News quickly spread round the hospital staff that I was no longer bed-bound, and it wasn't long before I was visited by the Physical Therapy department, whose job it was to make me hate the Physical Therapy department. Through a series of gothic abuses involving ropes, pulleys, weights, portable stairs and actual personal insults, they helped me understand why our Department of Homeland Security has issued its new directive: Going forward, we will no longer be using the term "Physical Therapy."

But I'm okay. Thanks to the top-notch hospital staff, I can walk. There's some kind of weird whistling noise, but I can walk. Also, if I stand outside when it's raining, I tend to get wet, but I'm told that's fairly common for people who've tried to head-butt a rock. And I still have an aversion to very tall things, like coffee table books and SUVs.

And if anybody bets you that I'll be parasailing to commemorate Memorial Day, you should definitely take the bet

"How long have I got, Doc"

"Ten. "

"Ten what? Months? Years? Weeks? "

"Nine...

Eight...

Seven...

Six... "

CHART TALK #1

Hospital Humor from "Dr. Jollytologist® (aka Allen Klein)

Hospitals are not exactly places that provide a lot of laughter. However, there is one source that does produce a lot of chuckles: the medical charts kept on patients. In the rush to write down a patient's condition, the healthcare professional often charts things which are ripe for humor.

Here are some chart excerpts that medical staffs have written on patient's charts:

- Patient has chest pains if she lies on her left side for over a year.
- On the third day, the knee was better, and on the fourth day, it had completely disappeared
- Discharge status: alive, but without permission.
- Patient was admitted through the emergency department. I examined her on the floor.
- The patient is a 90-year-old white female with multiple medical problems as well as severe osteoporosis that has been living with her daughter.
- The patient left the hospital feeling much better, except for her original complaints.
- I saw the patient today, who is still under our car for physical therapy.
- Patient left his white blood cells at another hospital.

- Patient was released to outpatient department without dressing.
- The patient lives at home with his mother, father, and pet turtle, who is presently enrolled in day care three times a week.
- The test indicated abnormal lover function.
- The patient is numb from her toes down.
- The baby was delivered, the cord clamped and cut, and handed to the pediatrician, who breathed and cried immediately.
- The patient has been depressed ever since she began seeing me in 1983.
- The patient said her neck was increasing in size where we took it off.
- I've suggested to the patient that he loosen his pants before standing and then, when he stands with the help of his wife, they should fall to the floor.
- The patient stated that she had been constipated for most of her life until 1989 when she got a divorce.
- Patient refuses an autopsy.

A hospital notice posted in the nurse's lounge said: "Remember, the first five minutes of a human being's life are the most dangerous." Underneath, a nurse had written: "The last five are pretty risky, too."

Shouldering the Burden
By Ernie Witham

My wife and I switched sides of the bed.

I know this might not seem like such a big deal, but we have had our own particular side of the bed for years. Just like we have our own pillows and pillowcases – as if everyone doesn't drool once in a while – reading lamps, reading material, and night stands. Hers is–was—the organized "doctor's office" nightstand. Mine was the nightstand that looked like the employee lounge at a tire and muffler shop.

A number of times over the years we have talked about mixing things up a bit—jokingly crawled into each other's spot and sniffed around a bit. And once, after several martinis and a particularly risqué Hallmark Hall of Fame movie, we even rolled over the wrong way to catch our breath and dozed off. We quickly switched back at first light and I ended up with two additional pillowcases.

But this time was different. This time I needed her side for medical reasons. See I had surgery on my right shoulder. Seems my rotator cuff was no longer attached to the bone. The doctor said it was an old injury most likely aggravated by years of column writing. Well, not the actual writing but the things I have to do sometimes to get material, like tubing behind a speedboat: "Look at me. Look at me. Ahhhhhh…"

And surfing: "I'm up. I'm up. Whoooaaaaa…"

And softball: "I got it. I got it. Ummpphhhh…"

And of course swimming in the pool with the grandkids: "Watch this! Double back flip, followed by a triple twist. "Sppplllllaaattt."

Even things like golf have aggravated my injury because of my steep swing plane that often ends a foot or so behind the ball, creating a divot the size of a condo lawn. And that's just when I'm putting.

So several weeks ago, after convincing me that spontaneous healing was doubtful and things were going to get worse, the doctor went in and reattached the tendon to the bone using a technique that involved drilling, trimming, pulling and stitching. Similar, I guess, to putting tufted naugahyde vinyl seats in a classic car. When I woke up he handed me a bill that will require I write this column for another 97 years, and then he fitted me for a sling that I'd have to wear for approximately six weeks or so.

Did I mention the fact that this was my right shoulder and that I'm right-handed? So I have had to learn to do all kinds of things with my left hand. Like brushing my teeth: "Kaaawwwkkkk. Kaaawwwkkkk."

Blowing my nose: "Whoops. Sorry kids."

Eating: "Excuse me, waiter? Can you take that string bean out of my nose?"

And certain other functions difficult to do with the opposite hand: "Excuse me, Dear can you…?"

"Not a chance."

But by far, sleeping has been the worst, especially with a sling on. It's kind of like being half man, half mummy. It has been particularly difficult in that I cannot turn over or move about. Plus my right arm was buried under a sheet, comforter, quilt, an ice pack and a few taco chip bags, and some of those same magazines from the employee lounge at the tire and muffler shop.

So, my loving wife felt bad and we switched sides so that I could keep my slinged arm outside of all that falderal, and so I could use my good arm to help me get up in the middle of the night if I needed to use the restroom.

"Excuse me Dear…"

"Still no."

Although I'm still a long way from normal – some might say that's always been an unattainable goal for me – I am on the mend and I now have a new appreciation for my limbs. Plus my wife and I are both getting used to our new side of the bed. "Right Dear?"

"It does help now that the smell of peanut butter and jelly has dissipated."

Plus, the doctor said he was pleased with the way surgery went and I could expect a full recovery, and if I ever wanted to put tufted naugahyde vinyl seats in my 1999 Mercury Mystique to give him a call.

A young female came to the ER with lower abdominal pain. During the exam and questioning, the female denied being sexually active. The doctor gave her a pregnancy test anyway and it came back positive. The doctor went back to the young female's room.

Doctor: "The results of your pregnancy test came back positive. Are you sure you're not sexually active?"

Patient: "Sexually active? No, sir, I just lay there."

Doctor: "I see. Well, do you know who the father is?"

Patient: "No. Who?"

Poker Face
Dawn Weber

The Christmas trees. The needles. They want me dead.

Yes, for the third time in my adult life, I've managed to sustain an injury from a holiday tree. This year, a thick pine needle has embedded in my finger. Won't come out. It will probably require medical treatment, just like the other two occurrences.

Not sure why the Christmas trees hate me so. I want an artificial tree, and lobby for it every year, but the husband likes "tradition" and all that happy horse-crap. So, every year a tree must slowly die in our living room, and every year, I sleep with one eye open. Watching, waiting... The first time a tree tried to kill me, I was fresh out of college, a young photographer in Warren, Ohio. Sporting my shiny new photojournalism degree, I had big dreams of taking award-winning photos in war-torn nations.

Instead, I covered pet-of-the week, ribbon-cuttings and holiday decorating contests.

Reality: Always a letdown.

One freezing afternoon, I arrived at a middle-aged woman's home to photograph her Christmas tree, for yet ANOTHER entry into yet ANOTHER decor contest. She was giddy at the thought of having her displays photographed for the competition.

"Oh GOOD! You're HERE! I have everything all lit up and ready to go!" she said.

"Great. Thanks," I said.

My eleventy billionth Christmas decoration photo of the week. It was hard to contain my excitement.

Ambling in, lugging my gear, I unpacked and began shooting her mammoth, long-needled holiday monster. She had many suggestions for good photos.

I had some suggestions for her…and what she could do with her tree.

Although I never said them out loud, the conifer must have read my mind. Because, as Crazy Christmas Lady yanked me around for yet another angle of her prized tree, it happened. Her arm, in conjunction with the evil tree, pulled back a long-needled branch and whacked me, full-force, in the eyeball.

AHHHH! NEEDLES in my EYE! Searing pain! Blinding bright light! Did I mention the NEEDLES in my EYE?!

You want Christmas? I'm pretty sure I saw Jesus that day. I know I said his name. And stuff.

Standing there, blind and gushing liquid from my eye, I heard Crazy Christmas Lady briefly ask if I was OK before dragging me to another angle of her tree. I faked a couple more photos, eye still weeping and blinded. I had to get away from CCL. Before I punched her.

One eye working, the other still flowing like a faucet, somehow I drove back to the newsroom. The boss took one look at my pummeled face and transported me to Trumbull Memorial Hospital, where I received the happy news that NEEDLES in my EYE weren't quite going to be enough that day. I had a scratched cornea and I needed a tetanus shot.

Hypodermic needles? Tools of the devil. Needles are not meant to insert in skin. I know this because every time I see a needle approach skin, I usually vomit and then promptly faint.

I told the handsome young (Single! I didn't see a ring! McDreamy!) resident that I really didn't need a tetanus shot.

"You know, I'm immune to Christmas tree germs, so I don't think…." I said.

But he was adamant in his mission to poke me. And not in any kind of fun way.

The nurse came in with the tray of NEEDLE.

"Oh Gawd, I'm going to throw up," I told Doc McDreamy. (Sexy! I bet he wanted me.)

"Get her a bowl!" said McDreamy.

And then it went black.

I woke up, drooling. (More sexy.) But - bonus! - I hadn't peed my pants. I was slouched in the exam chair, with McDreamy and the nurse restraining me from falling on the floor. They had used my blackout as an opportunity to poke me, and not in any kind of fun way.

I learned many valuable life lessons from this incident. Such as forever-after avoiding Trumbull Memorial Hospital and McDreamy. Also how to file a Workers' Comp claim.

But holiday trees and needles weren't done with me yet. No sir.

A few years later, as a young wife (sadly, not married to McDreamy. Although I bet he wanted me - drooling blackouts - hawt!), I was running speaker wire around the living room after Christmas when I stepped on glass from a broken Christmas tree ornament. Teeny-tiny slivers of German glass, poked directly through the ball of my right foot.

Hurt like a sum-bitch.

I did the smart thing: ignored it. Eventually, I figured, the glass would work its way out.

For three years, I tried this "ignore" tactic. Three years of step STAB step STAB step STAB.

Those Germans can make some glass.

So I limped around with piercing, festering glass in my foot instead. I limped until I could limp no more, and finally, I made an appointment. One sure to be filled with NEEDLES.

My doctor, (sadly, not McDreamy. Who surely wanted me…) was a nice man, very interested in my photography career.

"Oh! You're a Photojournalist! Cool job! You're lucky!" he said.

Looking at the doctor, assessing his probable $250,000/year salary compared to my $20,000, I said nothing. I also thought it best not to mention my standard Christmas tree and ribbon-cutting assignments. I was busy hoping "Cool Job!" status would keep me from the doctor's hypodermic NEEDLES.

But it was not to be.

Out came the tray of NEEDLE to numb my foot. Long….sharp….NEEDLE!

"Ahhhhh! That's too big!" I said.

"This will just numb you! Just a pinch!" said the doctor.

Sure as hell didn't feel like numb. Or a pinch. The hyperventilating began….the nausea….and he jabbed…repeatedly. There are more than 7000 nerve endings in a foot. He hit them all."AHHHHHHHHHH!! OWWWWW!!!!!" I screamed.

"Photojournalists are supposed to be tough! You'll be OK!" he said.

And then it went black.

When I came to, my foot was cut and bandaged, the glass was out, and the doc was standing over me.

"Man. I thought photojournalists were supposed to be tough," he said, shaking his head. He pulled off his gloves, and walked out the exam-room door.

You know, he was right. Photojournalists are tough. Also, all my experience with trees and needles and doctors has made me really smart and medically astute.

So I think I'll just let this third Christmas tree injury, this year's NEEDLE in my finger, alone.

I bet it'll work its way out.

When the government gave out brochures on specific diseases, I felt the one on Herpes was more suitable for an examining room, so I put it up on the wall. It was in the style of questions, followed by answers. I finished examining a small boy, and was talking to his mother. He had just started to read, so looking at the brochure, he slowly read out a heading,

"When can I have sex again?"

There was an awkward pause, then his mother said, "You sound just like your father!"

Your Recent Stay With Us
Barb Best

Dear Patient,

You've just stayed with us, and we'd like you to share the ~~traumatic~~ details of your ~~horrific~~ experience with us.

Please tell us how we can make your visits even more comfortable and convenient by taking our five ~~hour~~ minute survey. After an agonizing stretch in the hospital, what's one more precious chunk of your time?

1.   Were the healthcare providers – even the snotty night shift nurses – reasonably attentive to your life and death issues?

2.   Did the nurse's button work? At least some of the time? And was she/he able to push your buttons consistently?

3.   Did ANY Doctor actually locate your room and say "Hi," "Bye," or "Boo?"

4.   Was English spoken? Understood?

5.   We are a smoke-free and sleep-free institution. Did hospital personnel respect this rule? The moment you drifted off from sheer exhaustion and acute illness, were you awakened promptly and deprived accordingly?

6.   Did you find the meals to be reminiscent of foul public school cafeteria food?

7.   When taking blood for labs, did you bruise a vivid black and blue and swell instantaneously? If not, appropriate force may not have been applied.

8.   When your chirpy octogenarian roommate went into cardiac arrest, did you jump in and help with the Code Blue? If no, why not? Every party has a pooper...

9.   If diagnosed with a terminal illness, were you satisfied with the manner in which the healthcare employee gave you the 411? And could you please pay the bill *now*. *Right* now, please.

10. Regarding your operation:

A) At any time during your surgery, did you wake up and scream bloody murder? Cry for your mommy? Text your lawyer?

B) Do you remember *anything*? God, we hope not.

C) Do you still have the proper limbs and organs attached? For instance, left leg vs. right leg; liver vs. kidney; eyeball vs. testicle.

D) If you croaked on the table, saw the light at the end of the tunnel, and came back anyway - fess up. We need to charge you an extra fee.

11. Was TV reception:

A) adequate

B) intermittent at best

C) horrible

D) a real pain in the rectum

E) What TV? I thought that was the drugs.

12. Yes or No: Were you sent home with prescriptions for lots of pretty little pills that cost a pretty little penny?

13. Are you enrolled in our "Frequent Pain" program? You can earn valuable points for discounts on disturbingly invasive procedures like an anesthesia-free endoscopy or a slow-mo lumbar puncture.

Thank you for sharing your comments and for visiting us with your escalating healthcare needs. Your feedback will help ensure that we continue to provide you with an exceptional patient experience.

The Shoo T. Menow Memorial Hospital
Customer Relations

A striking redhead walks into the examining room and says, "Doc, I hurt all over."

"Please show me where."

She pokes her finger into her upper arm and says, "Ouch".

She gently touches her thigh, "Ow!"

She taps the top of her head, "Owwww!"

She scratches her ear, "Oweee."

The doctor looks at her a moment and says, "You're not really a redhead, are you?"

"No," she says. "I'm blonde but I dyed my hair because I'm sick of people thinking I'm stupid. How could you tell?"

"Your finger's broken."

THE FICKLE FINGER OF FATE

Decision of Terror
By Chris McKerracher

Recently my entire fiber has been swirling with a veritable smorgasbord of negative emotions; steaming bowls of fresh fears along with platters of sphincter-clenching panic and tureens of the purest terror and trepidation. You see, I finally have a date! No, not with the red-headed girl I had a crush on in high school, a la Charlie Brown, but for a hip replacement. It was like getting a recall notice from the original Manufacturer.

Besides bad puns and worse jokes, it seems defective hips run ...or rather, limp through my family's genetic make-up. Our hips, apparently, have the durability of a soda cracker in the clothes dryer. Of all the qualities displayed by my father, I must say that replacing important parts is not how I envisioned following in his footsteps.

What is causing me the most consternation, however, is that the last time I talked to the sawbones (I suddenly find I hate that nickname for a doctor) I was asked to make a rather difficult decision. He needed to know whether I want to be knocked out for the procedure or just have a spinal block applied so I would remain awake throughout the de-boning.

Like everything in life, both options have their points; good and bad. Initially, I was leaning towards the spinal block thingy despite my understandable aversion to people screwing around with my backbone. It's been often pointed out I don't have much of one to begin with and letting somebody jab a caulking-gun-sized needle into it may not be my best course of action. Still, the surgeon had said it was the healthier choice, as recovery time is shortened and I wouldn't be as apt to die on the operating table. (!) This counted for a lot in my books as surviving to old age is way up there on my "things to do list", along with cleaning the gutters and tidying the garage. I realize my kids believe I've already have made the first goal but then, they think thirty is old.

Since doctors are handing out more new hips than door-to-door religion enthusiasts hand out magazines, I've been able to talk to a number of ...er... hipsters about their experiences. Without exception the ones that had the "epidural" procedure ended up with the medical practitioner missing the main spinal doohickey and the patient having to endure the most skull-crushing headache of all time. As their cranium pounded away, they could listen to the bone saw at work and feel the doctors physically bending and twisting their body around as they applied force to complete the installation.

That is the gist of what most said but I could only bear it for so long until I had my fingers in my ears going, "BLAHBLAHBLAHBLAHBLAH" to drown out the horrible fate that awaited me.

Okay, that's it, I thought, this spinal block idea was against my religion. I am, after all, a practicing Coward. I realized my only option was to be knocked out. I should add I call it "knocked out" as opposed to Cupcake who calls it "Being put to sleep". This is unsettling. "Being put to sleep" is what we called it when we euthanized our dog when she got so sick. When I pointed this out to Cupcake, she just smiled wistfully and changed the subject.

I was happy to have arrived at a decision on my fate. Being rendered unconscious seemed to be the perfect solution to my problem. I was relieved I didn't have to give it another thought until I watched a program on CNN regarding a phenomenon called "Anesthesia Awareness". In the piece, people claimed they were traumatized from waking up on the operating table and felt every slice of the scalpel but, being so immobilized from the anesthetic, they couldn't call for help.

My Plan B suddenly became Plan Big Fat Chicken. "Now, now, honey," Cupcake tried to console me, "This sort of thing is very rare."

"Oh yeah?" I challenged, "It's already happened to me. Remember when I had that camera go down my gullet and they gave me those drugs to make me 'compliant and forgetful'? Remember? I mentioned to you that drugs like that could really help our love life."

"I remember," agreed Cupcake, "I said if I got my hands on some, I would have every chore done immediately and all you'd know is that you woke up feeling sore every morning."

"But they didn't work one hundred per cent!" I proclaimed, clutching her arm. "I recall waking up and fighting the doctors when they were trying to shove the tube down my throat! I shouldn't have been able to remember that but I do!"

"Calm down," urged Cupcake, "They do thousands of these operations now and they usually go off without a hitch. How often do you hear about scandals at a hospital?"

I looked at her balefully.

"Maybe now is not the time to answer that," she continued hurriedly. "But really, Dear, if people were waking up willy-nilly during operations, I think it would be in the newspaper. Since when do you believe anything on CNN?"

"If only I could be as sure as you," I moped.

"Well, how about this, "Cupcake offered. "I can prove I believe you have nothing to worry about; that I'm not just saying it."

"Oh?" my eyebrows shot skyward. "What proof?"

"I didn't buy extra life insurance," she pointed out.

I felt so much better.

"Gosh, Honey," I grinned. "You're the best!"

A woman goes to her doctor who verifies that she is pregnant. This is her first pregnancy. The doctor asks her if she has any questions. She replies, "Well, I'm a little worried about the pain. How much will childbirth hurt?" The doctor answered, "Well, that varies from woman to woman and pregnancy to pregnancy and besides, it's difficult to describe pain."

"I know, but can't you give me some idea?," she asks.

"Grab your upper lip and pull it out a little..."

"Like this?"

"A little more..."

"Like this?"

"No. A little more..."

"Like this?"

"Yes. Does that hurt?"

"A little bit."

"Now stretch it over your head!"

Waiting for Dr. Godot
Jim Mullen

It's nice that Dr. Godot has a whole room just for waiting. It's so convenient. But it makes you wonder. If he called it the "Wasting Your Valuable Time Room" would his patients sit there so willingly? Calling it a waiting room makes it sound as if waiting is the most normal thing in the world that we could be doing with our time. We're not fuming, we're not steaming, we're not twiddling our - thumbs because it's a waiting room—not a fuming room, not a steaming room, not a twiddling-our-thumbs room.

There must be some really thoughtless doctors out there who take patients as soon as they show up at their scheduled time and don't give them any time to wait. But as soon as they are found, they are drummed out of the profession. Of course, it's not just doctors that make us wait. Airports are composed almost entirely of waiting rooms. They have acres and acres of waiting rooms. The waiting rooms are so humongous they have book stores and restaurants and souvenir stands and coffee bars in them. If the airlines really thought every flight would leave on time do you think they'd build such gigantic waiting rooms? Maybe the ticket price for air travel should drop each hour you have to wait. Wait one hour, ten dollars off the ticket price, two hours, you save twenty dollars and so on. For every hour you sit in the plane on the tarmac, fifty dollars off the ticket price. Under this system, most of us could make money by flying.

My appointment with Dr. Godot was for two o'clock; I still haven't seen him and it's now three o'clock. But if I had shown up at three o'clock I would have missed my appointment. I would have been late. That seems so one-sided. If I have an appointment with Dr.Godot, why -

doesn't Dr.Godot have an appointment with me? Oh sure, I understand that there are emergencies. I watch those hospital shows on TV. Well, I used to, but not anymore. It's too unreal.

On TV, entire families walk right into the Emergency Room without waiting; Mom, Dad, five or six children all wailing and screaming, "Don't let her die!" She has a bad case of psoriasis. The psoriasis family never fills out a form; they never wait a minute. The doctors on television all look like fashion models. Dr. Godot looks like Jack Klugman.

On television no one ever waits. A show called WR - wouldn't stand a chance. Who would want to watch a big room full of people moaning and sneezing and bleeding from the forehead and NOT being treated?

At least Dr. Godot tries to class up his waiting room and make it comfortable. He hangs pieces of fine art, and the chairs are big and soft. I even know what he does in his spare time thanks to the magazines scattered around. Godot subscribes to High Class Ski Resorts, Exclusive Golfing in Europe, Expensive Antiques Monthly, Cigar and Wine Bore, and Cayman Islands Tax Shelters.

There is a very fine reproduction of a large, ancient Etruscan vase in his waiting room placed between two - chairs. It's waist-high. The classy effect is spoiled, however, by the hand-printed note taped above the vase that says, "This is not a garbage can!"

How can they be so sure? Maybe that's exactly what the Etruscans used it for. Garbage pick-up on the ides and nones of every month. The Etruscans are probably having a good laugh that Godot paid six grand for it at auction.

Finally at three-thirty the nurse told me the doctor would see me now.

"I'm so sorry about the delay," said Dr. Godot, "but there was an emergency. A man collapsed out at the golf - course."

"Is he all right?"

"I suppose so; EMS took care of him. But it held up our foursome for an hour."

A man and a woman were waiting at the hospital donation center.

Man: "What are you doing here today?"

Woman: "Oh, I'm here to donate some blood. They're going to give me $5 for it."

Man: "Hmm, that's interesting. I'm here to donate sperm, myself. But they pay me $25."

The woman looked thoughtful for a moment and they chatted some more before going their separate ways.

Several months later, the same man and woman met again in the donation center.

Man: "Oh, hi there! Here to donate blood again?"

Woman: [shaking her head with mouth closed] "Unh unh."

Caffeine and Boobs
E.C. Stilson

It all started one day when a fabulous friend of mine called. "I've been nervous to tell you something," she said. "My boobs have been swollen and I thought something was wrong."

My heart dropped. We've been friends for years and I love that woman. The thought of her having breast cancer tied my intestines in knots.

"Well, the only reason I told you now is because I realized I'm okay . . . I've done some research online. If you drink too much caffeine, it can make your boobs swell and cause intense lumps and pain."

"Caffeine," excitement laced my voice.

"Elisa? Are you listening? This isn't a good thing . . . except that I'm not drinking as much Diet Coke and I'll be okay."

"I'm so glad you're all right AND that you've given me the key to happiness."

"What are you talking . . . oh no," she paused. "Don't do it."

"But I'll get bigger boobs." I smiled, concocting the best plan ever!

Too bad she's a genius who's NEVER wrong because now my boobs hurt and they're still just an A minus! It was time to see a doctor.

So, instead of buying a push-up bra, I had a nice long bath before going to the doc. I was glad about that, after the nurse led me to the room and said, "Just undress completely and he'll be right in. It's time for your yearly exam."

I walked into the room, but there wasn't a gown on the table. The woman shut the door.

What kind of place had I gone to? Did they just expect people to get naked and sit there like a Playboy model? I wasn't into that, so after thinking awhile, undressing and getting dressed again, I opened the door. "Ma'am? There's no gown."

That woman seemed miffed, actually miffed. She looked at the doctor and said, "Oh, silly me. I'm so sorry. We've had a very busy day with all the labors and deliveries and things."

The poor woman. Was it putting her out to do her job?! I clutched the ugly fabric and went back into the room. "Just flip this light when you're ready and he'll be right in," Miss Miffed said.

I tied the gown, flipped the switch and after sitting there a minute, I smelled something. I sniffed, once, twice. My eyebrows sunk in worry and I glared at my stupid, FAVORITE shoes that I've had forever. Once I made the mistake of wearing them without socks—a mistake I'll never make again. I'd worn them to the doctor's office and not worried they'd make my freshly washed feet stink even through new socks. Too bad I'd been wrong. I knew I was in a pickle. No one wants to visit an OB AND have stinky feet!

The metal sink gleamed at the edge of the room; that's when I got a brilliant idea. I could flip the switch off and quickly wash my feet. I couldn't imagine how awful it would be to have some womanly exam done while my feet ruined the air. So, that's what I did. I'm sure my bare butt shone through the gown as I rushed to the switch and flipped it off. I pumped the soap, rubbed it into a nice lather and held my left foot at the sink's level.

It was a bit hard balancing on one foot, so I hopped a couple times and some water and suds fell on the floor. I kept glancing at the door to make sure the switch was still at an "off" position. But the whole time I had this bad feeling like someone was watching me. Maybe it was God or some angel who laughed at my soap-loving expense. I didn't know, but I hurried so fast I had one foot cleaned in no time.

I smiled in victory. That foot smelled like it belonged to Hera herself and the other just needed to be washed. I held my right foot up, the leg closest to the door, and that's when the door opened.

I stared in horror as that young doctor walked into the room. He was just a bit taller than me. I'd heard women say he's handsome, but I must disagree. His arrogant eyes hit the floor, then the gap in my gown, then my foot that I'd pulled near the sink. He gulped hard and clutched his stupid clipboard.

I froze with my leg up—like I was playing freeze tag for crying out loud! I couldn't move. All I wanted to do WAS DIE!

"Oh, my . . . Ummm . . ." He looked away. "Wow, so there's some water on the ground."

Water? Was that all he'd noticed? Talk about "The Guinness' Book of World Records"—he should be in it for the understatement of the millennium!

I got nervous and when I get that way, I start cracking dumb jokes. It's my defense mechanism.

That's why instead of putting my foot in my mouth, I put it on the ground and said, "Since you've already seen everything should we still go ahead with the exam?"

He cleared his throat, not even showing a smile; I suddenly knew I hated that arrogant Peeping Tom. The whole thing was his fault. I hadn't flipped the stupid switch! Now, 'hate' is a strong word, but he wasn't doing anything to make me—the customer who WAS right AND sudsy—feel better. "If I could just get you to sit down, then I'll check you out . . . I mean no, not like that. I wouldn't check you . . . I'll do the exam."

Could he just kill me with the pelvic exam cone and get it over with! I really did want to die. Of course I knew the idiot wouldn't check me out! Why had I worn those dumb shoes?

"Do you have any concerns other than," he looked at my feet, "a swollen breast?"

Since the first joke hadn't worked and I was nervous, I started blabbering on. "Well, since I had my last baby, I've been feeling a bit depressed."

He pulled his glasses down. "How often?"

"Once a month." I acted serious, and then a clownish smile lit my face. He didn't even chuckle! The least he could do was politely laugh. I wanted to stick it to that man who'd just been part of my most embarrassing moment ever.

"You're going to be fine, just fine." But he looked at my feet again. What the hell—it was worse than when you talk to a guy who won't take their eyes off your lips!

So, the exam sucked—I won't lie about that. I've never been so mortified in all my life, but I did cross some hurdles today; I know I don't have cancer, I have been drinking too much caffeine, AND I no longer have those shoes I used to love. I'll never wear those to the OB again because wearing stinky shoes to the doctor's office IS NOT the best thing since Double D's.

Medical Terminology 101
Public Domain

Benign.....................What you be after you be eight
Bacteria...................Back door to the cafeteria
Barium.....................What doctors do when patients die
Caesarian Section...A neighborhood in Rome
Cat Scan...................Searching for kitty
Cauterize..................Made eye contact with her
Colic.........................A sheep dog
Coma........................A punctuation mark
D&C.........................Where Washington is
Dilate.......................To live long
Enema......................Not a friend
Fester.......................Quicker than someone else
Fibula.......................A small lie
G.I. Series...............World Series of Military baseball
Hangnail.....……......What you hang your coat on
Impotent......……......Distinguished, well-known
Labor pain....…….......Getting hurt at work
Medical staff...…......A doctor's cane
Morbid...........……......A higher offer than one bid
Nitrates...................Cheaper than day rates
Node........................I knew it
Outpatient..............A person who has fainted
Pap Smear..............A fatherhood test or speaking ill of
one's father
Pelvis..........……...........Second cousin to Elvis
Post Operative........A letter carrier
Recovery Room......Place to do upholstery
Rectum...........…........Darn near killed 'em
Secretion...….............Hiding something
Seizure................…....Roman Emperor; to whom the
loyal fall down & give an *"All Hail"*

Tablet....................A small table
Terminal illness....Getting sick at the airport
Tumor..................More than one
Urine....................1) Opposite of mine
(2) what the ump says when you make it to home plate
Varicose...............Near by, close by

A man is lying in a hospital bed with an oxygen mask over his mouth.

A young student nurse comes by to sponge his face and hands.

"Nurse," he mumbles from behind the mask, "Are my testicles black?"

Embarrassed, the young nurse replies, "I don't know, I'm only here to wash your face and hands."

He struggles again to ask, "Nurse, are my testicles black?"

Again the nurse replies, "I can't tell. I'm only here to wash your face and hands."

The charge nurse passes by and sees the man getting a little distraught, so she marches over to find out what's wrong.

"Nurse," he mumbles, "are my testicles black?"

Being an experienced nurse, she is undaunted. She whips back the bedclothes, pulls down his pajama trousers, moves his penis out of the way, has a good look, pulls up the pajamas, replaces the bedclothes, and announces, "Nothing is wrong with them!!!"

At this the exasperated man pulls off his oxygen mask and asks again, "Are my test results back?"

'Roid Rage
Linton Robinson

Every bar has a guy like Ronnie Hershfield who talks all the time but nobody pays any attention to him because he's never right about anything. Except that one time when I had to admit he got it right and wished to hell he hadn't.

I'd been having trouble getting dates lately. Getting anything, if you want to come right down to it. Which is why I was taking the ballroom dance class. And it looked like that might be working out, because there was this girl. Dianne: lightly built, pale blonde, cute, smart, good dancer. Better than me, for sure. But she accepted every time I offered to be her partner for the hustle or whatever disco number they were playing on the boombox in the Wilsonian ballroom, just off the University of Washington campus. And I was getting the impression she might say yes if I asked her out, try out our steps at one of the discos over on Shilshole Bay.

But meanwhile, I had a pain in the butt. The kind you can't really scratch. I'm pretty sure it wasn't the dancing that flared up my hemorrhoids, but who knows. Maybe Saturday Night Fever wasn't completely a mental state. But the inflammation was driving me bats and I was finding that the amazing substance Bio-Dyne, much ballyhooed ingredient of Preparation H, was not drawing the body's own healing oxygen to the site of the irritation, as advertised. Or at least not enough. I had no idea what you did about inflamed rectums, but wasn't too wild about finding out. I sure wasn't going to ask my roomies, a bunch of Mopar freaks who would call me Hemi-Head to the end of my days.

University Hospital was an impressive sprawl of erudition and healing energy (not to mention government grants and femme-nazi nurses) but I figured it would cost me and besides I worked in the parking kiosk and didn't want to be recognized.

So I slouched into the on-campus student clinic, an old lump of brick known as Hall Health, but more commonly referred to as Hell Hall. Where I ran into the usual stalling and form-filling and ID card checking. When I finally got to talk to anybody not glued to a monitor screen, it was a dumpy gatekeeper who looked like she might race dogsleds for fun. And of course, she had to ask me what my complaint was. I'd been afraid of that. I guess I mumbled "Got hemorrhoids," because she looked up and said, "Beg your pardon?" with this really snotty look. She could beg all she wanted, I would never forgive her. So I said, crisp and well-enunciated, "My asshole is sore and red."

Oddly that didn't make her any less snotty, but I'm sure she was secretly pleased. So she dumped me in a rickety chair (like I really wanted to *sit*) over by other old Alaska-Yukon surplus chairs mostly occupied by people adept at not making eye contact. I didn't care if they knew about my "presenting condition." I would happily have allowed them a visual inspection at the slightest provocation. The term "pain in the ass" for general irritation was not chosen loosely.

When the lanky Kasbekistani doctor, holding a clipboard as if to deflect gunfire, finally called my name, I had to tear myself away from reading the regents' report in a two-year old alumni magazine. Then I had to follow him down into an examination room where he sat and I stood while telling him about my symptoms and suspecting I was actually giving him an unpaid ESL class.

But what he lacked in English skills, bodside manner, and personal grooming, though, he more than made up for in sheer techno-geek bravado when I managed to inform him of my delicate condition.

I had to drop trou, of course, and he squinted at my annular deformation, making professional tsking sounds in Jihaadistani or whatever, then invited me by gestures and facial grimaces to shuffle over to the big steel contraption that dominated the room, but which I had managed to ignore, thinking it was a Xerox machine engineered by The Borg. With the air of a conjuror, he produced a heavy black cable with an attached keypad, exactly like some James Bond arch-villain would use to control whatever doomsday machine he was about to fire up and start dooming with. He thumbed the remote with moves obviously honed by years of geek gaming, causing a little tilt-out jump step to extrude from the infernal machine, square and sharp-cornered, but padded like those kneeling platforms in Catholic churches. Gradually (and with a growing horror) I came to understand that he expected me to kneel on it and lean my torso down on top of this suddenly ominous cube of enameled steel. I knelt on it and he did another thumbdance on the remote, causing hydraulics to whine and whir, thus raising me to the proper height to lean forward, face down on the (sparsely) padded top. Not that it's that horrible to kneel on a servomechanism like that, but just wait, will you? He produced wide straps from the side of the machine, reeling them out without even a fiendish chuckle, then using the airline seatbelt style fasteners to clip them over my back and behind my thighs, then clenching them down tight like load binders. I was, at that point, if you are up to picturing it, bare-assed and spread into what biologists refer to as a "presenting" position, and helplessly restrained. And in the hands of some foreign weirdo with hornrims. Not a position that engenders security, trust, and well-being in the average male. Hell, the average anything. But it got worse.

I found out what the whole hydraulics bit was all about (if I'd thought about it, it would have seemed an expensive overkill way of tipping a knee tray out, but the Bond baddy imagery had lulled my impressions) when he did more fiddling with his remote. I was hoping there were no buttons for "Mute" and "Lube" and "Enable Reach-Around", but what it had was even more sinister, to one in my predicament: the examination table started to rotate forward, while also rising and lowering experimentally like a slow-motion mechanical bull ride for pederasts. I was being tipped head down, thus lifting my rear components to a more convenient height and accommodation. "Convenient" and "accommodating" not being terms we like to think of in relation to our already inflamed orifices. I was thinking this machine was designed by feminists to get even with males for gynecology stirrups when it shuddered to a stop, leaving me doing an impression of a howitzer aimed at a distant foe.

I told the doc I wanted to get a franchise for these dire devices, sell them to rich Arabs, but I don't think he caught the nuances. Instead he made my day by telling me that he wanted one of the med school interns to come in to assist and "observe the procedure". Again, "proceed" is not the sort of highway sign one likes to envision slapped up on their chocolate highway, but there wasn't much I could do about it, strapped down with my butt aimed up into easy reach. I learned that in a position like that it almost doesn't matter how many people are standing around rubber-necking, evaluating, and commenting on parts of you where until recently the sun never shone. Notice I said "almost"?

Because when the door opened and the intern entered (accompanied by the ominous rattle of autoclaved stainless steel implements of procedure on a polished metal tray) I could see by peering back past my legs that she was female. Imagine my joy. On the other hand, that much less likely to dabble in sodomy. The doctor, being even more clueless than he looked, *introduced* us! Hard to say which of us would be less likely to want to acknowledge the other in that situation, right? Well, it turns out to be an easier choice than you'd think.

You've probably already figured out what I said to her, haven't you? Which was, "Uhhh, hi, Dianne."

I'd forgotten that my dream dance date was in pre-med. Told you she was smart. I'm not the world's glibbest conversationalist, but I've always been a little proud of my next line, as she stood there with no idea of how to deal with our unexpected "face to face" meeting. Which was, "Hey, you want to go dancing at Spinnakers Friday night?"

So what does this sordid incident have to do with Ronnie Herschfield being right for once in his life? Well, a week before my adventure in rectal surgery and affairs of the heart he'd been telling me, "Know your problem with women? You always come on to them ass backwards."

Doctor says, Good news, bad news
Good news, your penis has grown four inches
since last exam
Bad news, it's malignant

Don't Be Fooled by the Cold, Blue Body
Mike Cyra

I didn't really like working as a Nurse's Aide in a hospital, up on the floors where all the sick people were. Nobody likes being in a hospital, and nobody really likes to visit people who are in the hospital. But I needed money to pay for my Emergency Medical Technician school, so you do what you have to do.

The upside of it was that I got extremely good at rapidly taking vital signs and assessing a patient's condition. Taking accurate blood pressures while a television or radio blares in the background, with loud people who don't want to be visiting someone in the hospital served me well down the road, in the world of emergency medicine.

The downside of it was that I filled more pitchers of pee in those six months than I have drunk pitchers of beer in my entire lifetime. Let me tell you something about smelling pee. There's OK smelling pee, and then there's pee that will curl your mustache hairs like a blowtorch cigarette lighter.

The stench somehow clings to your brain so badly that you get treated to little whiffs of it two and three days later when you're trying to make out with your girlfriend. Brief fits of gagging ruins all chances of getting to second base.

Upside, I dated some nurses that re-wrote the book on nasty. Downside, a lifelong aversion to visiting people in hospitals.

One of my duties as low man on the totem pole was to go to each room every hour and take pulses and temperatures and blood pressures and check the bags of pee hanging off the side of the bed, and clean poopy beds and poopy people.

I always worked the night shift since I went to school during the day. So I got used to waking up people who were sound asleep or shlocked to the gills on narcotics so I could annoy them to no end.

Nothing wakes a patient up in a pissy mood better than someone moving around the garden hose that's shoved up your wee-wee into your bladder.

Actually I found that the two times I've been catheterized wasn't that bad. It's the epitome of laziness. Gotta pee? Ahhh…taken care of!

I found the concept of effortless urination relaxing. I've often thought about how nice a handy-dandy catheter would be on football Sunday. Drink beer all day, never miss a play and never have to get up from your chair. Just drink, pee, watch football and hold the remote.

The only preplanning necessary would be to have a small refrigerator filled with beer within arm's reach and to leave the front door unlocked so the pizza delivery guy can get in and "deliver" the pizza to your chair. Who knows, if you tip him enough, he might even empty your pee bag into some empty beer cans, which would buy you enough time to watch a couple more games.

Obviously, I've thought this through more than once.

So there I am, in the hospital, going from room to room annoying people. One of the last rooms I walked into had an older gentleman in the bed who was sound asleep.

He was a nice old man who I had talked to many times on previous shifts. I even ran my Sunday catheter football idea past him. He suggested that if I could somehow incorporate cheerleaders inserting the catheters, then I might just have a million dollar idea.

He looked so peaceful sleeping that I didn't want to disturb him. I gently lifted his arm up and wrapped my blood pressure cuff around his arm. The part of my brain that was actually functioning noted, "Boy he sure feels cold. I'll make sure and snuggle his blankets up around him before I leave so he stays all toasty warm."

I put my stethoscope in my ears and began pumping the blood pressure cuff up, watching the needle on the gauge rise. Then I slowly released the air in the cuff and waited to hear the heartbeat that would give me his blood pressure. And I waited. I watched the needle in the gauge spin down to zero.

This wasn't unusual. I thought maybe he was hypertensive. Patients with high blood pressure sometimes make it difficult to hear the heartbeat. You simply pump the cuff up higher and take the blood pressure once more.

Again I stood there and watched the needle spin down to zero without hearing any "lub-dubs" through my stethoscope. As usual my brain was on it. "Huh, having a little trouble getting a pressure on him. Wonder why?"

My hand instinctively moved down to his wrist to feel for a pulse. My fingers searched around and couldn't feel one. I thought, "Hm, maybe he's hypotensive." Patients who have low blood pressure sometimes make it hard to feel a pulse.

After my fingers groped around his wrist a few more seconds, a thought slowly began to creep into my head, "Well this is kind of unusual."

I looked up at his face and I could have sworn he was wearing bright blue lipstick. I waited for my brain to process this information, throw out the lipstick scenario and come to a more educated explanation of what I was seeing.

I bent over him and leaned my head in sideways until my face was directly in front of his. "Hello?" I sounded like a nosey old woman knocking on a neighbors screen door, trying not to sound snoopy by half singing the word, "Hell-low?"

I reached up and lifted one of his eyelids open and repeated the stupidity, "Hell-low?"

I figured why stop there. When you're on a stupid roll you have to go with it.

I reached up with my other hand and lifted his other eyelid. We were now staring at each other. I sang, "Anybody home?"

The image of Little Red Riding Hood staring at the Big Bad Wolf laying in bed wearing granny clothes flashed into my head and I thought, "My what big pupils you have!"

I let go of his eyelids and they stayed there, open, his eyes staring straight through me at something on the wall behind me.

I pulled the covers down and put my hand on his chest. Everything was coming together for me now and I verbalized the last piece of the puzzle. "People aren't supposed to be this damn cold!" I nervously scanned the empty room around me and whispered, "This guy's dead."

Jumping into action, I quickly retrieved my blood pressure cuff from his arm and stuffed it in my pocket. Then I pulled the blankets up just under his chin and smoothed them out all nice. I even folded an inch of white top sheet over the blanket and smoothed that out until it looked peaceful and perfect.

Using the same quiet walk the Pink Panther uses; I headed for the door. I didn't need anyone walking in on me while I was trying to sneak out of some dead guy's room.

Once in the hallway, I went straight up to the nurse at the desk and said, "Hey ah, room 302, I ah, I'm thinking he's not doing too well. I had a hard time getting a blood pressure on him."

Without looking up she said, "Yea, that's probably because he's dead, Mike. Been dead for a couple of hours. Just waiting for the family to come up and see him."

I was thankful she didn't look up at me because I didn't have control of my facial muscles and had no idea what expression I was making.

When you feel that stupid, it's hard to react with any grace sufficient to restore your dignity. A man has to know when to cut his losses and just walk away. I slowly started meandering away from the desk saying, "I'm just gonna, you know, start my rounds again."

She compassionately kept her head down and said, "OK."

Desperately trying to make a graceful exit I asked her, "Any other dead people you wanna tell me about?"

I saw her head shake and heard a muffled, "Nope." And with that, I melted into the walls and simply disappeared.

Two kids in waiting room:
Why are you crying?
I'm here for a blood test and they're going to cut my finger
The other kid starts crying.
Why?
I'm here for a urine test.

A Smashing Success
Dorothy Rosby

Thanks to my first kind and efficient mammogram technician, I do not fear the mammogram. I hate it, but I don't fear it. And I continue to have mammograms faithfully whenever the calendar and the latest medical advice suggest. I suppose that makes my initial mammogram a smashing success! Sorry.

I was already tense when I arrived, so I almost canceled when the receptionist asked for an emergency contact. What kind of emergency could there be during a mammogram? She assured me it was just to be on the safe side, but she didn't say whose safe side.

I felt better when she asked if I had implants. "Oh! Do I look like I have implants?" But she said she had to ask everyone that.

After filling out my paperwork, I met the woman who would be doing the procedure. I've had a few mammograms since that first one—though it seems like a lot more. And each time I've been helped by very caring technicians. It seems like the sort of job bullies would apply for—and men. But I've met neither at what I, being a journalist, refer to affectionately as "the Press Club."

The technician gave me a little poncho to cover myself as well as a wipe to remove my deodorant. I didn't think this was the kind of experience I should go through without deodorant. But she said it could show up on the pictures, and she didn't think I'd want to do retakes.

Then she explained what she was going to do, which was essentially flatten my bosom in a giant vice, though she didn't put it like that. She remained determined, but kind throughout this procedure despite my complaints and the fact that I wasn't wearing deodorant.

She never once said, "Don't be a baby," or "Is that all you've got?" She was gentle and sympathetic, but that didn't stop her from doing what she had to do. And what she had to do was put my breast in the vice, tighten it, then go out for coffee.

I'm JOKING! She was actually very quick. I only had time for two worries. First, would I faint? I reassured myself that I probably wouldn't. And even if I did, I couldn't very well fall to the floor—not with my chest in the press like that.

Secondly, would I "bounce back" after my mammogram? I know it sounds crazy, but I was convinced everyone back at the office would be able to tell I'd had a mammogram just by looking at me.

And then it was over. Really the best thing about mammograms is that they're fast. Oh yes, and they save lives. But that's really all you can say for them.

After that first mammogram, the technician gave me a gift—a bottle of hand lotion with the logo of the Press Club on it. It was thoughtful, but I think a tee-shirt would be a more appropriate gift, not to mention, a better way to advertise. On the back it could read, "I did the right thing. I had a mammogram!" Then on the front it would say, "I wasn't always this flat."

(Dorothy Rosby is up-to-date on all routine check-ups and on her immunizations as well.)

The Patients Of Job
From "HMO Fails" Reality Show Pilot

These are all GENUINE replies from patients asked why they needed an ambulance to and from hospital.

- I am under the doctor and cannot breathe.

- I can't walk to the bus stop and my wife is bent.

- I can't breathe and haven't done so for many years.

- I want transport as bus drivers do funny things to me and make me feel queer.

- I am blind in one eye and my leg.

- I live five miles from the hospital and the postman says I should have it.

- I have got arthritis and heart failure in both feet and knees.

- I must have a man as I cannot go out or do up my suspenders.

- I cannot walk up a hill unless it is down and the hill to the hospital is up.

- My husband is dead and will not bring me.

- I cannot drive a car as I have not got one.

- I hope you will send a man as my husband is quite useless.

I can come at any time to suit you, but not mornings as I don't feel too good. I can't come on Mondays or Wednesdays as the home help comes, and not on Fridays as the baker calls for his money. I can't come on Tuesdays as my sister calls.

World Wide Worry
Janet Nicholson

The Internet has opened a whole New World for the hypochondriac. Whereas medical knowledge was formerly limited to magazine articles, health books and know-all neighbors, the Web is a virtual Disease City, providing a magnitude of frightening medical possibilities.

Hypochondriacs do not worry alone, they also diagnose for friends and relatives, which is why Health Sites receive tens of millions of hits annually, and may indicate that hypochondria is contagious.

It is fortunate that my Auntie Phoebe is not still around to log on. Auntie Phoebe suffered from every disease known to woman (and, occasionally, man). She was jealously possessive of her infirmities. Whatever ailed friends, neighbors and relatives, Auntie Phoebe was also a martyr too. This included problems with her 'prostrate'. We even invented a disease – retillion – that she swore had left her kidneys permanently impaired.

Auntie Phoebe prided herself that her symptoms were more severe, unusual or previously unknown to that disease. She liked nothing more than to baffle the doctors. Papers were going to be written about her, like dispatches from the front. She was a challenge to medical science.

Auntie Phoebe's unhealthy interest in medicine began in her younger days when she spent two years as secretary to a gynecologist. The doctor's handwriting required Auntie Phoebe to look up spellings in a medical dictionary – which, happily for her, also provided a description of the disease. Her escalating medical knowledge sometimes emboldened her to pre-empt the doctor's diagnosis, and patients would enter his office secure in the outcome of their visit. It was not long after that Auntie Phoebe's employment was terminated.

When she left the practice, Auntie Phoebe had amassed a sizable quantity of medical journals, an out-of-date Mims, and the happy knack of steering every conversation down the avenue of medicine. She gathered together symptoms like a data bank. A veritable www.tellauntyphoebe.com, she could surf Mims—on the hard drive inside her cranium—for answers to any medical conundrum.

If someone arrived at the comforting conclusion that his or her medical problem would disappear if certain vitamins were imbibed, Auntie Phoebe would gleefully trawl her memory, and quicker than any search engine would suggest the symptoms indicated a more menacing disease. But she was also www.auntiephoebewillfixit.com.

Auntie Phoebe knew about party power long before Tupperware. Like a dating agency she would match her friends' symptoms and then hold morning coffee pill swaps. Pills for a bad back would surely help ease the pain of sciatica. A nervous disposition would benefit from anti-depressants. As far as we know, no one died as a result of her ministrations.

Aged 92, Auntie Phoebe died peacefully in her sleep. Nobody would have been more surprised than she next morning.

At the wake, her family ceremoniously threw the Mims on the fire. I thought it was a pity. I had been hoping to look up causes for my sore throat.

Never mind there's always the Web.

I Must Be Concussed
Cammy May Hunnicutt

I've been reading a bit about concussions lately. How the schools and leagues are trying to increase awareness of concussions. Which is really great, because I am here to tell you that when you get concussed the main thing you run short on is awareness.

First time I was made aware of concussions was by this geekoid resident in a Montgomery hospital. Not my usual kind of conversation. There was nothing going on before it, you know? Like I just woke up and it was the first day ever and this nerd in a white coat is asking me what my name is. And I'm just staring at him. He gave me this look and started scribbling something down on a clipboard. I was going to just slap it out of his hands and start asking some questions of my own, since I seemed to be in bed alone with this guy who practically had "Roofie Rapist" written on his forehead and God knows what he had all that creepy stainless steel paraphernalia for.

Trouble was, I couldn't move my hands and couldn't think of any questions. If I could've, the first one would probably have been, "What's my name?" Which is what he was asking me. That's how it was. Kind of scary. But also sort of existential. Not that I knew existential from a differential. I was still a high school sophomore. Not that I knew that, either. What I knew was, I had to pee. So I did. Looking back on it, it would have been better to get out of bed first. It got rid of Dr. Dork, though.

The next conversation, sometime the same year, was with some sort of psych nurse. But she had that same obsession with names, which was starting to weary me. Everything was wearying me silly, truth be told. It was a good thing I was hospitalized because I was sick of everything. She was like, "Can you remember your name?"

And I said, "Of course." Pretty patronizing. But my hands were still constrained to the bed. By which they mean "tied up with plastic cop laces". Apparently being unaware hadn't kept me from whuppin' on a few staff. I was nobody to mess with in those days, let me tell you. Tomboy hockey horror from hell. And now I was imprisoned in their clutches with no underwear.

So I said, "Cammy May." Duh. It was written right on my wrist.

"Good." Simpery beaming. "And your other name?"

Uh. "May."

"Good, good. And your family name?"

Family. Whoa. That was a good one, all right. Not the sort of answer you want to rush in on. Uhhhhh. "Flora. Beth. Daddy. Mama."

By the time she left we had shared a few things. Like my whole name, what country I was in, what was the year, who was President. She told me what day it was, but she was probably lying. Complete bitch.

Meanwhile I was getting a massive headache, which also kind of felt like a hangover. They were concerned about this and eventually told me a bunch of crap about it in Latin and Klingon or something, probably more lies. Blood building up in my head somewhere. Likely story.

About five minutes later, I was talking to some other goober in white and this time I had a bandage on my head that Little Orphan Annie's bodyguard would have loved. And, I later realized, no hair. I was kind of a pioneer in that whole skinhead thing for chicks.

And guess what they were yacking about? My name.

But this time, which I finally figured out was different from the last time, was even more different because I was doped to the gills to keep me from awareness of the pain that results when you saw somebody's head open so you can get under the hood and change the oil and check the points.

I realize this sounds awful, but I didn't mind (especially during the doped-up part, when I wouldn't have minded being dragged across Georgia naked by rabid wolverines). But a couple of things totally sucked.

For one, it turned out I'd been cold-cocked during a game. When they told me that, I was dumbfounded (it's really easy to be dumbfounded post-concussion on opiates, actually) because it was really central to my identity that *I* was the one who did the cold-cocking, thank you very much. I swung a mean hockey stick and was the enforcer for a team that was undefeated at that particular time. I mentioned that and they got even more concerned and told me it had been a volleyball game. I got my heel stuck in the net and fell on the back of my head. How humiliating was THAT? How many volleyball concussions have there ever been? It's like blowing out your knee playing ping-pong.

So what I had at that point was a spazz injury, followed by bed imprisonment and blackout, followed by utter stupidity. But it still wasn't as bad as the video.

The first time they let the members of my family--you remember the Whatstheirnames?--come in to see me, I'd just talked the token nice nurse into some pain meds because I'd tried to get out of bed and whanged my knee something awful. The expression "feeling no pain" took on new meaning, although it escaped me at the time. I was right back to do-it-yourself existentialism. Turned out my evil brother Powell brought a little video cam and taped the whole thing. Which went something like:

Somebody: Hi Cammy, do you know us?

Me: *Know* you? I made you! I love you! You're all just beautiful. Thank you, thank you.

Sister Flora Lee: How are you feeling?

Me: I'm feeling happy, girl. I feel happy and horny and honey. I feel like waffles. Or wait...French toast. *Oui, oui, slante.* That's a French toast. (garbled laughter)

Little Bethany: Does it hurt?

Me: Only hurts me when I cry, bunny rabbit. Nothing hurts because nothing gives. See? Hurtin' is for certain and pain is for gain. Come here, give me a hurt, honey. I mean a kiss. I said gimme a hurt! That's just so hilarious. (More crazed laughter)

Mama: Don't worry, sweetie lamb, you're going to be okay. This won't...

Me: I'm okay. I'm okie kay with a bouquet of Tokay. It's cool, Mama, I'm happy as a hog eating goose guts in the shade. Y'all are so sweet. Just look at this little kewpie pie right here. (Some scuffling around to get Bethany's cheek out of the painful pinchers of my fingers, which some idiot had unrestrained.)

Brother Powell: Can you remember anything?

Me: I remember everything. EVERYTHING! (Singing to the tune of the "Barney" song) I remember you, you remember me, now we both have HIV. I remembered to forget so it's all good, bitch.

Mama: Camelia May, you watch your language.

Me: But Pow *is* a bitch, mama. He's a bitch, bitch, bitch. Ding dong, the bitch is dead, ding dong, the bicked ol' bitch is dead. I love that bitch, though. I love that dirty old bitch, don't I?

There's more. It just goes on and on and on. It's been years and I've still never managed to find that tape and destroy it. And gradually it all came back. Memories of everything except whatever happened between walking into the gym and waking up in bed with Dr. KaDorkian giving me the eyeball. Vocabulary. Pain. Reflexes. Normal thoughts. Well, same as.

My overall impression of concussions and Demerol: not a dime's worth of difference. Except I don't think anybody would get addicted to concussions. Not on purpose, anyway.

A young man about eight years old complaining of abdominal pain was brought to the emergency room by his mother. I interviewed him while his mother patiently looked on. As part of my assessment I asked him "When was the last time you had a poop?"

He looked at me with a blank expression. Thinking he hadn't heard me I repeated, "Did you have a poop today?"

Once again he looked at me with a puzzling question and turned to his mother, she responded

"The doctor means a *bowel movement*, son"

DOCTORS YOU DON'T WANT TO GIVE YOU YOUR PROCTOLOGY EXAM

Dr. Dre

Dr. Pepper

Dr. J

Dr. Seuss

Dr. Bunsen Honeydew

That weird doctor with the butt fetish

THINGS YOU DON'T EXPECT TO SEE WHEN YOU WAKE UP FROM YOUR LONG COMA

Your wife kissing the doctor

Horse and jockey

Your daughter, now 77 years-old

Walking dead zombies

Ted Nugent

St. Peter at the Pearly Gates (really confusing for someone coming out of a coma, to be sure)

INDICATORS THAT YOUR OPTHAMOLOGIST IS BLIND

Tells you to read the letters on the far wall. Points to the nurse's bosom.

Asks you to try on a new pair of glasses. Hands you his sack lunch.

Says he's going to perform a color blind test. Puts tongue depressor in your ear.

Tells you he's going to check for pupil dilation. Flashes light on nearby janitor closet.

Asks you to follow his finger with your eye. Places finger on nurse's bosom.

WHAT I FOUND IN A HOSPITAL STORAGE ROOM OTHER THAN WHAT YOU SEE A LOT ON TV HOSPITAL DRAMAS, THAT IS, HOT DOCTORS HAVING SEX

Bandages

Latex gloves

Chemical wipes

Tongue depressors

Surgical masks

Janitor masturbating

UNFORTUNATE ITEMS E.R. DOCS HAVE FOUND INSIDE PATIENTS' RECTUMS

Fruit

Matchbox car

Fountain pen

Rolling pin

Lumber

Thimble

Canoe

Wormhole into a 4th Dimension

Corsage

Penny

Remote Control

Despair

Detroit Lions Playbook

Golden raisins

Fur ball

Hula hoop

Pitching wedge

Freezer burn

Melancholia

Spoon

Hole punch

Ottoman

Bell

Chicken wire

Menu

Vegetables

Turkey baster

Poop

Magic wand

Stick of butter

Onyx

Ken doll

Skeleton key

Small intestine (of someone else!)

Griddle

Peanut brittle

Bouillon cube

Newt

Windshield wiper

T-square

Suppositories (still in box!)

Baton

Tire iron

Thumb tack

Jelly

Sleeve of Ritz crackers

Ranch dressing (still in bottle!)

Tusk

Daguerreotype

A second rectum

THINGS YOU DON'T WANT TO OVERHEAR
FROM YOUR DOCTOR TALKING TO THE NURSE
AS YOU SIT THERE ON THE ER BED AWAITING
WORD ON WHAT HAPPENED WITH YOUR
SIMPLE SPRAINED ANKLE

Bloody discharge
Polyp
Horse tranquilizers
Chlamydia
Cancerous urethra
Call the morgue

WAYS PORN MOVIES STARRING HOT NURSES ARE NOT REALISTIC

Lots of manual stimulation, but not a lot of insurance card information changing hands

Lots of oral sex, but not a lot of intravenous feeding

Lots of Kama Sutra positioning, but not a lot of adjusting the hospital bed to see TV

Lots of panting, but not a lot of puking

WAYS SPONGE BATHS ARE SEXY

Hot water
Sudsy soap
Bedsores
Oh, not bedsores. That's gross.

The New England Journal of Medicine reports that 9 out of 10 doctors agree that 1 out of 10 doctors is an idiot.
Jay Leno

Shuffling Cards at Work - Deal Me Out
Dan Burt

In a recent scientific survey, all Americans said they would rather be attacked by a rabid badger than sign greeting cards at work. Granted, the sampling size of the survey was a bit small (me and Max, my coworker and racquetball partner), but I think the results represent a fair assessment of the situation.

Every week, I am inundated with cards for every conceivable occasion: retirement, birthday, sympathy, get-well, acquittal. Last week, I signed a card for someone's second cousin's godmother's pug for graduating obedience school (valedictorian no less!).

I never know what to write on the accursed cards, either. Most of the time, I don't know the person (or animal) that well, if at all. Usually, I play it safe with the standard phrases: "Wish you well," "My condolences," or "Good luck with that." Once, when I discovered a card on my desk one morning, I quickly scribbled "Congratulations" and passed it on. That afternoon, Lance from sales came to my office, jerked me out of my seat with a firm handshake, and pulled me close for a spine-crushing embrace.

"Thanks man," he whispered in my ear. "You're the only one who knows how I really feel." Later, I discovered I'd signed a sympathy card acknowledging the passing of his mother-in-law.

Some people have no problem writing heartfelt passages. One disgruntled coworker wrote on the retirement card for one of our managers:

"Having reached the twilight of your mortal existence, please accept my congratulatory sentiments as you prepare to leave this ennui-inducing hellhole and make your way to paradise and your seaside condo. I remember well our initial acquaintance— sitting in orientation one score and five years ago, two young, creative lads lactating ambition and motivation galore, until all was slowly suckled from us by this godforsaken bureaucracy, a bureaucracy that nursed relentlessly, leaving our teats of aspiration depleted and withered, never to plump anew. Anyway, good luck and watch out for hurricanes."

The disgruntled worker was also a bitter, failed novelist.

If I know the person well, I may add an encouraging personal note such as I did on a recent get-well card for my friend and racquetball partner, Max:

"Sorry about the mauling. Don't worry; my Aunt Melvina suffered a similar fate with a raccoon. She regained most of her mobility and her scars are barely visible in low light. Hang in there; I'll reserve a court for us."

Max had landed in the intensive care unit after simply sticking his hand in his mailbox, retrieving a package of Gevalia coffee, and flinging it at a rabid badger weaving across his front lawn.

I visited Max in the hospital to deliver his card and conduct my survey. Though he was completely bandaged, in traction, and unable to speak, I could see in his eyes he was enjoying his respite from having to deal with the cards at the office. Thus, I am confident in the accuracy of my survey's results.

SPECIAL DELIVERY

How to Get Appendicitis
Kate Heidel

Just my luck: not long after my appendix was removed, science decided that this vestigial wormy thing had a splendid function after all. Whereas once it was branded a freeloader that did nothing until it ruptured and took your life hostage, the appendix was now being credited with producing helpful bacteria only when you needed some. Well aren't we clever.

So I hope you'll get to keep your bacteria-producing Worm of Wonders, but be aware that you stand a 1-in-500 chance of contracting appendicitis. If your little fella goes to the dark side, allow my experience to be your guide to:

The Best Method of Achieving Appendicitis without Dying and thereby receiving my bonus guide to: *Getting a Good Week of Legitimate Sick Days Out of It*

First, remember that the very earliest sign of appendicitis is unusual indigestion. Now I, who was born with indigestion and will die with a Rolaids in my mouth, assumed I would never be able to distinguish the harmless variety from the kind that leads to possible deadness. But, amazingly, I did: it was extra knotty and growled something from *Les Miserables*, which I never could tolerate.

I also managed to perform my self-diagnosis on a Sunday afternoon—more on that later. For now, get thee to an emergency room.

If you are female, I'm afraid you're going to have to undergo additional testing to ensure that your symptoms have not arisen by way of a feisty uterus. Do try to get the E.R. staff to send you off for that test *before* the MRI of your appendix. Because the MRI requires a prep consisting of fruit juice mixed with a laxative that would clean out an elephant. Yes, long after the staff doesn't need you to "void" anymore, you'll still have a stomach full of turbo-charged cranberry juice blasting you into the biffy even though the official Time for Pooping has elapsed.

Before you are wheeled to the pre-op room, pull out your cell phone and call your boss's work number, which you happen to have on you for just such a delightful occasion as this.

"Hello, Boss?" you'll say, "It's Sunday night and I thought I'd let you know that I'm about to undergo surgery for acute appendicitis. So I won't be in tomorrow. Actually, hold on, yes, the doctor is telling me I probably won't be in for the rest of the week. They have to put me under now. Bye."

It feels so good to make that call you'll almost forget your appendix is trying to kill you.

If you are still conscious when they wheel you into the operating room, do not concern yourself with the profusion of surgical instruments. Yes, there is enough gleaming metal to equip a M.A.S.H. unit, but you are getting five days off of work, so keep your priorities straight.

I myself could not possibly have been less concerned, for a previous ankle surgery had introduced me to a lovely drug called Versed. Ask for it by name! Versed makes you feel so carefree that you'll wish you were having surgery every day for the rest of your life just so that you could ask, "May I have a little Versed, please? I'm feeling kind of anxious."

Those are the magic words. Soon, someone in scrubs will come padding over and cheerfully empty a syringe into your i.v. line, rendering you a very silly person in love with all humanity.

For as long as you remain hospitalized after surgery, you will be reminded by a variety of admiring personnel how incredibly "hot" your appendix was. Not hot like Heidi Klum, I'm afraid, but more like a worm so red and swollen it practically pulses on the verge of rupture. You weren't eating anything just now, right?

My wormy thing didn't quite achieve the ultimate State of Hotness, though—a scenario breathlessly described by a nurse who had been lucky enough to witness an appendix rupture right in the surgeon's hand immediately after removal. Wow! That's James Bond, brink-of-death hotness. I bet James could have substituted that for a kill and still earned his "00" status.

Personally, I'd rather get the sick days

The doctor approaches the man in the waiting room with that "bad news" look and he stands, very attentive. "How'd her exam go, Doc? Is she all right?"

Shaking his head the doctor intones, "Your wife has acute angina."

"I know," the guy smirks. "And a nice set of tits, too."

The Missing Vagina Monologues
Deb Claxton

I had to stop watching Dr. Oz because the show was too depressing. Apparently everything I'm eating, wearing, and doing will kill me - "Donuts: death traps with icing and sprinkles" or "Wearing Spandex will shorten your life span."

The final straw came when I watched an episode of Dr. Oz called, "Use It - Or Lose It." I thought he was talking about calf muscles. Boy was I wrong, he was talking about sex organs. Yikes, I lose my car keys and reading glasses all the time. I didn't know I could lose my vagina! After the show all I could do was think about the following horrifying scenario:

"Attention K-mart shoppers, someone found a fossilized vagina in aisle 7 would the owner please report to customer service immediately!"

I couldn't sleep at night because I was worried about the condition of my vagina. I was afraid to go to my OB/GYN.

"Put your feet up in the stirrups please. This will feel cold (are they storing their speculums in the freezer compartment?) Let's just take a look. Oh dear. This isn't good. I'm afraid I have some bad news. Your vagina has vacated the premises. There's nothing left but a sign that says, "Prime space available. Call Lady Parts Real Estate."

I know what you're thinking, "Why didn't you pay more attention to your vajayjay?" It's not like I wanted to live like a nun. I don't have a husband, boyfriend, hook-up buddy, significant other, or insignificant other. I live in a small town. There aren't any eligible men. Everyone is too young, too old, married, gay, married and gay, or on parole. I don't want a one-night stand. I don't want to date young men. There's too much work involved in trying to look 20 when you're 50. That only leaves old men. I tried to pick up an elderly widower at the local nursing home.

"I hear you're single, Melvin. Would you like to go to dinner and see a movie?"

"What?"

"I said dinner and see a movie."

"What? You're a sinner and you want me to see your boobies! Alright I'll take a look."

"NO!!! I SAID DINNER AND A MOVIE!"

"Okay. I'll just go put in my dentures then we better skeedaddle. I want to get to the all-you-can-eat buffet before 4:00. Afterwards we can go see that new Buster Keaton movie."

Obviously that didn't work out and the situation looked hopeless until I read some good news online. In the near future scientists will be able to clone body parts for routine transplants. That includes sex organs. In 30 years, I'll be able to get a brand spanking new vagina. Hopefully by then I'll have a boyfriend.

First the doctor told me the good news: I was going to have a disease named after me.
Steve Martin

Specialists' Opinion on ObamaCare
Country Club Poll

The American Medical Association has weighed in on the new health care package. The Allergists were in favor of scratching it, but the Dermatologists advised not to make any rash moves.

The Gastroenterologists had sort of a gut feeling about it, but the Neurologists thought the Administration had a lot of nerve.

Meanwhile, Obstetricians felt certain everyone was laboring under a misconception, while the Ophthalmologists considered the idea shortsighted. Pathologists yelled, "Over my dead body!" while the Pediatricians said, "Oh, grow up!"

The Psychiatrists thought the whole idea was madness, while the Radiologists could see right through it. Surgeons decided to wash their hands of the whole thing and the Internists claimed it would indeed be a bitter pill to swallow.

The Plastic Surgeons opined that this proposal would "put a whole new face on the matter". The Podiatrists thought it was a step forward, but the Urologists were pissed off at the whole idea.

Anesthesiologists thought the whole idea was a gas, and those lofty Cardiologists didn't have the heart to say no.

In the end, the Proctologists won out, leaving the entire decision up to the assholes in Washington.

Gut Surgery is a Pain in the Butt
Stacey Hatton

If you have experienced abdominal surgery of any form, it is questionable which is more challenging: the actual surgery or the entertaining pre-operative bowel prep. Yes, the Mount St. Helens of Uranus. The Projectile Maximus-Cheekus-Interuptus or as the classy Hollywood types call it…a little colon cleanse. Let me tell you, if I had to perform this procedure on a regular basis, there would be no "star" on the sidewalk hollering MY name!

When you look up Magnesium Citrate in a drug reference book, there is a picture of the devil pointing his finger at you and laughing his…let's stray and say, head off. It's that Beelzebub elixir which cleanses your colon to make things spick and span for your surgeon and nurses. Heaven forbid the staff be grossed out by a speck of poop when they are gutting you open like a trout.

Thankfully, the bottle-from-hell did the trick and I was as clean on the inside as I was ever going to be. The only problem with this method is I had used two rolls of toilet paper, half a tube of Desitin Rapid Relief diaper cream and had developed a hemorrhoid the size of Lithuania. Pre-surgery jitters were gone. I was never more ready to be anesthetized to escape this burning asteroid which had turned my shiny heinie into an engorged orangutan's tuchas that Birute Galdikas would have begged to photograph.

5:30am: hospital arrival time …TOO early.

My husband had no difficulty finding prime parking at the hospital. Peculiar. Since it was offensively early and no lines were tripping me up, the tornadic hospital staff swept my driver's license and health insurance card through the scanner - and before I could click my heels together, I was stripped down and donning the largest patient gown Oz could summons. Granted I live in the one of the top five fattest cities in the country, but this pastel muumuu swallowed me and my hemorrhoid without flinching.

As I was sitting on a gurney behind a curtain, awaiting my next rapid-fire order when a nurse flew in (I'm pretty sure she had landed her bubble outside my curtain). She asked me a gazillion questions and right before she happily stuck the largest bore needle in my arm she asked, "They had you urinate in a cup, right my dear?!"

First of all, who are they...the Lollipop Guild, flying monkeys? And secondly, "No." to the pee question. *Glinda the Good Witch, RN was appalled!* "Well, you better get in that bathroom STAT and tinkle before I get you hooked up to these IV poles."

So I hiked up my wearable tent, making sure to swathe my orangutan protuberance and sneaked away to christen a cup. When I entered the bathroom, there was the typical plastic basket next to the toilet containing the usual suspects: cups with orange lids, a permanent marker for labeling the cup, and wipes.

After having several children, I am a pro at peeing in a cup and the "clean catch" method. I could probably teach it to newly pregnant women in my sleep – but that would be weird and unacceptable at most OB/GYN offices. I won't go into the details of how I performed the duty, but let's just say, I succeeded with one minor glitch. Ms. Hemorrhoid wasn't happy.

Remember those TV commercials where the hemorrhoid was shown on fire...or was that athlete's foot? Whatever it was, my butt was ON FIRE! Those obstetrical wipes are supposed to be soothing - cooling even. What was going on down there? So I grab another wipe and try to read the print. Damn my aging eyes!! That's why I didn't read it in the first place, I can't see without my readers. If I squint real hard...stretch the arm...ah, yes...focus...ANTI-ADHESIVE WIPES!

Oh, thank the Lord for the word "ANTI!" I almost glued my butt shut! What if the moronic person who filled that plastic basket with anti-adhesive wipes had put in ADHESIVE wipes?! I was one step away from having one less hole! How do you explain that one to the nurse? *Excuse, me. Nurse Glinda? We have a little problem that might slow down your morning schedule...*

Well, at least that urine-covered permanent marker was accessible so I could have written a note to my surgeon on my abdomen.

"Doc, while you're down there...how about a favor? I glued my butt shut in an unfortunate "pee in the cup" accident. Don't mention to Nurse Glinda. Not sure she's a good witch."

What is the difference between a hematologist and a urologist?
A hematologist pricks your finger.

Cut Here to Open
Robert G. Ferrell

It started as an occasional inexplicable tingling in my left hand: the kind you might get from leaning on an elbow for too long or raising your arm above your head while a TSA agent calls his buddies over to snicker at your prosthetic armpit. The tingling periods grew longer and more frequent and spread upwards, accompanied by muscle pain. Eventually my entire left arm was tingling and cramping almost constantly. To reduce the incredible discomfort I was forced to keep lofting it in odd positions: a mobile 'impatient New Yorker hailing a cab in the rain' performance art piece.

To say that I don't find visiting my physician—or any physician at all—to be a particularly pleasant experience is equivalent to stating that the Tuskunga event did not, on the whole, contribute to the health of the surrounding forests. I'll wait while you look that one up.

Treatment stage one was physical therapy. Physical Therapy is where people go to have their bones, muscles, tendons, ligaments, joints, and cartilage manipulated in ways Nature never intended or even realized possible. Most of my sessions consisted of having various anatomical features in my back and shoulders subjected to the sort of ultrasound energy marine engineers use to diagnose structural failures in deep-sea drilling platforms, followed by what I was repeatedly assured was a 'massage.' I was lying prone on a table at the time, in a poor position to observe the proceedings, but it felt as though the therapist had taken an axe handle in each hand and was attempting to play my spinal column like a xylophone. The lower notes were a bit on the flat side at first, but by the time she finished they were a quarter-step higher in pitch, presumably as a result of fragmentation.

I underwent this self-financed pummeling twice a week for five weeks, at the conclusion of which donating my body to science was looking more and more like an attractive option. By which I mean: it hurt to breathe. It hurt when someone in the same room with me breathed. It hurt when I encountered water vapor. The vibration from sunlight hitting the window jostled me unbearably. Cosmic rays left livid bruises. It was the worst of times on the best of days.

Next, my medical team decided to try pharmacology. Lots of it. So much pharmacology, in fact, that had I been summoned for one of the random drug tests to which I am subject as a condition of my employment, just handling the plastic cup with my urine in it would have made the nurse start giggling uncontrollably and then belt out the complete soundtrack to Wicked whilst dancing on the nearest examination table wearing only her stethoscope. Sadly, no summons was forthcoming.

Having never partaken of illicit psychoactive enhancement in my life, I had no prior voyages of discovery against which to compare what I experienced the first time I choked down the cornucopia of pills, caplets, and capsules I was ordered to ingest. It was like swallowing all the parts leftover from a dozen plastic model kits. The narcotic pain reliever hit first, followed by the muscle relaxer and the tranquilizer. The rest, some of which I swear the Internet said were for topical veterinary use only, added color, texture, and fractal geometry to the phantasmagoria.

I've watched my fair share of movies and television shows in which hallucinatory experiences were portrayed, but none of them do the real thing justice. Compared to what I went through, Altered States was an after-school special. To begin with, hallucinations are not limited to the visual and acoustic organs. No. Everybody gets to play, right down to the lymph nodes and hair follicles. Having a drug hallucination is like suddenly finding yourself in a dream where your familiar universe has been liquefied and odd things are continually crystallizing out of that solution. At the same time your ability to judge distance is severely impaired, except that from your point of view it is the concept of linear measurement that has gone haywire. Objects you've possessed; nay, cherished, since childhood taunt you by changing size and morphology arbitrarily. Odors come and go, as well, most of them grossly inappropriate for the current milieu. I smelled tea rose and skunk in quick succession, for example, while perched precariously on the rim of my continually shape-shifting bathtub. Later I was standing at the nearby toilet when it began to shimmy and waver. I had to expend considerable concentration to track its movement well enough to do my business without excess spillage.

My sense of touch also took a terrific thrashing. I picked up a plastic CD case at one point only to fling it to the floor when I realized it had scaly skin and was wriggling in my grasp. I'm pretty sure a nearby coffee cup with penguin feet chuckled.

The daily stoning ritual went on for some time, although I did acclimate somewhat after a while. My wife was driving me to work and back, thankfully, or I might have taken a wrong turn and ended up in downtown Atlantis. My fellow employees regarded me as a semi-domesticated rhinoceros wandering around the office. They were congenial but circumspect and I caught the occasional glint of fear in their eyes. I'm sure some of the reports I wrote during that period were quite entertaining to read, and will doubtless be used as evidence if I'm ever brought to trial under a charge of non compos mentis.

The third bodily assault upon my person disguised as treatment was the ever-popular series of steroid injections. While this phrase calls to mind an athlete injecting himself surreptitiously in the thigh with powerful strength-enhancing elixir before competing in a major sporting event (gambling he won't get drug tested), it's actually a far cry from what I went through.

My steroid injections, in contrast, resembled one of those procedures you read about in history books that evil military doctors performed on captive test subjects. They plunked me on a hard metal table and folded me into a variety of positions until they found the least comfortable one—where I was lying on my side crushing my hip bone and arm with no place to put the other arm, with my neck bent almost at right angles to the rest of my spinal column—strapped me down, and gave me a 'mild sedative' that relaxed me into hysterics.

Now the doctor pointed one of those fluoroscope machines (the ones they use at some airports to check passengers for lethal weapons like bobby pins and paper clips) at my neck and theoretically referred to it while he guided a hollowed-out knitting needle as close to my spinal cord as he could without actually piercing it (piercing incurs a fifteen-yard penalty and loss of down). Once in position, he squirted in roughly a quart of the same stuff unscrupulous trainers use to keep horses running as long as possible after they're injured (just before they're made into glue and pet food). When I woke up and stopped screaming they slapped a bandage over the hole and sent me home. After three of these thrill rides I concluded the (mis)treatments were having no appreciable effect on me, apart from instilling a strange craving for alfalfa and sugar cubes.

By this time I'd been mauled by a family practitioner, a physical therapist, a pain specialist, two rheumatologists, and two neurosurgeons. The first neurosurgeon examined me, then decided my insurance was too much of a hassle and there was nothing he could (i.e., was willing to) do for me. The rheumatologists thought I might have Lupus (nada), deficiencies of Vitamins D and B12 (true), fibromyalgia (inconclusive), and rheumatoid arthritis (mildly positive). They also sentenced me to a couple of truly diabolical tortures called a 'Nerve Conduction Study' and 'Electromyogram.' I won't go into the gruesome details of these atrocities other than to say they involve many strong electrical shocks and then being stuck with a lot of needles simultaneously. I fully expected to find bolts coming out of my neck afterwards.

The second neurosurgeon took one look at my MRIs (these entail lying for half an hour in a tube where you have just enough room to breathe and listening to what sounds like several dozen dump trucks full of crumpled sheet metal repeatedly crashing into and grinding against one another) and told me I needed surgery* immediately.

*Surgery: an invasive medical procedure, usually conducted under local or general anesthesia, the mere anticipation of which reduces a well-adjusted, confident adult to a sniveling mass of self-pitying gelatinous substance.

My surgical ordeal began at the ungodly hour of 4:00 AM, when I had to get up and shower, making certain to wash my neck for the second time with a special (and no doubt ridiculously expensive) soap because there's no way it could get dirty again between there and the hospital, an hour's drive away. By 5:30 I was undergoing the admissions process, where a pleasant young man with glasses explained to me in a congenial but business-like manner that a gentleman with several diplomas was going to cut me open and I might expire at any point during the process. He asked me if I wanted them to give me blood if I needed it. That, to me, is akin to asking an airline passenger if she wants the pilot to avoid hitting any mountains that might pop up in their path. I replied, "Yes, I'd consider it a personal favor if they'd replace any blood they might accidentally spill while filleting my cervical vertebrae. Exsanguination would play havoc with my retirement plans." I could visualize the event: "Scalpel. Sponge. Suction. Oops. Better get me some blood. No, no: bring the whole bucket. And some super glue."

By 6:30 I was naked except for a hospital gown that didn't contain enough fabric to make a decent doo rag, lying on a gurney with an IV needle jammed into the back of my hand and taped so thoroughly in place I thought they might be expecting rough seas on the way to the O.R. Every few minutes a nurse, surgeon, radiologist, and even one guy who looked like he might have just stumbled in to the pre-op suite looking for a public restroom but who turned out to be my anesthesiologist, came by to ask me if I had questions, explain the insane tortures they were going to inflict upon me in matter-of-fact, dismissive language, and then, with sadistic gleams in their eyes try to reassure me that it was a routine procedure. So is euthanasia, I thought.

The neurosurgeon banged his head pretty hard on a cabinet in a brief episode of karmic vengeance that cheered me a bit until I realized that this was the same guy who was going to be rooting around in my neck in a few minutes with extremely sharp implements. Concussion was probably not going to improve his surgical technique.

Now came the interminable waiting game, which at least gave my wife time to run out to the car to fetch the cervical collar we forgot to bring in with us. The surgery was supposed to start at 7:00, but it was close to 8:00 when finally I was wheeled away to the abattoir. The last thing I remember was the homeless guy telling me he was going to add something to my IV drip to relax me. It relaxed me like an Acme anvil to the parietal lobe.

I woke up wearing the aforementioned cervical collar and a heavy bandage on my throat just above a tube that emerged from a hole in my neck and led to a translucent alien cocoon taped to my stomach. My throat had been reamed out using a mining drill bit and then coated thoroughly with ouch-flavored yuck. The nurse handed me a plastic mixing bowl containing a sample of every pill in the hospital pharmacy and told me to take them. I took them and set them on the table next to my bed. She put hands on hips (I presume they were hers; the light wasn't very good) and scolded me. "You need to swallow all of those." I peered into the bowl at Mt. Pharma again. "Wouldn't it be easier just to slit open my stomach and drop them in? I mean, there's bound to be a scalpel close by and you've got plenty of bandages. No one would have to know. You could hide it under the drain pan."

In the end—at least it felt like the end—I ingested them. Swallowing was an art lost to me in my post-surgical state, so I forced them down my throat employing the Johnstown Flood method. It worked, after a fashion, but the pill-propelling tsunami combined with constant intravenous hydration created a whole new dilemma: my bladder suddenly remembered what it was there for and began complaining in strident tones I could not ignore. I was still connected to various machines that went 'ping' (and sometimes, in the middle of the night when I was trying to get in a few minutes of shut-eye between nurse attacks, 'sproing' or 'thunk'), so traveling to the bathroom even were I capable of ambulation simply wasn't practical. Instead, I had to balance precariously against the railing of my hospital bed and relieve myself into a receptacle the design of which suggested it was originally intended for sampling ichthyoplankton.

I wobbled there as the forces welling up inside me grew beyond the reasonable containment point and discovered to my consternation that not only was I denied swallowing, but neither could I pee. My body's response to surgery was apparently to close its borders to all traffic, in or out.

Once the urine expulsion cycle had begun, however, something had to give somewhere. I pushed and strained with so much force I was afraid the pee might back up into my IV line. Finally I managed a dribble that barely exceeded the rate of normal nocturnal condensation. The associated pain, however, indicated I had ejected a portly and actively struggling hedgehog.

After a few hours reliving myself got easier, although for a while I was considering trying to divert the flow to my sweat glands. After all the painkillers I'd been given, that appeared to be a perfectly sensible alternative to my obstinate urinary tract. I wondered why no one else seemed ever to have tried it. Lying in a hospital bed listening to your spouse sleeping peacefully in a chair while you bounce back and forth between being delirious from pain and stoned out of your gourd patch is a perfect breeding ground for thoughts you probably should not think:

If colonoscopy looks at your colon, why doesn't laparoscopy look at your lap?

Why are there nurse sharks but no doctor sharks?

If leaving the hospital is being 'released,' why isn't entering it being 'caught?'

Eventually I got better at hiding the fact that I was stoned and they let me go home, but I had to wear the cervical collar that made me look like a failed Michael Jackson costume for over a month. My cat avoided me when I had it on, but the pain and tingling are gone. Best of all, I now contain not only two clumps of bone from dead people but two titanium plates and eight titanium screws as well. I guess I'll just have to check 'other' on those demographic questionnaires, since 'Zombie Cyborg' isn't usually one of the choices for race.

When the zombie apocalypse comes, in fact, I'll have a wider menu choice than most of them. I can run on brains or batteries.

A nurse asked the patient, "So how's your breakfast this morning?"
"It's very good, except for the Kentucky Jelly. I can't seem to get used to the taste," the patient replied.
The nurse asked to see the jelly and the woman produced a foil packet labeled "KY Jelly."

Butt Smoke
Mike Cyra

Warning!

If your life revolves around eating, cooking, growing, touching or looking at cauliflower, STOP HERE! DO NOT READ FURTHER.

If you choose to continue reading, do so at your own risk. I will not be held responsible.

Another Warning!

Wait at least two hours after eating to read this story. Be prepared to not eat, drink, smoke or have sex with anything for up to six hours AFTER reading this story. Longer if you have a vivid memory and are unable to block-out unpleasant mental pictures from your mind.

Really, really Serious Warning!

This story is absolutely, positively, NOT for children to read. That is, if you ever want them to eat certain vegetables, sleep without nightmares, not be a bedwetting freshman in college, or have a life-long phobia about what comes near, or in contact with their bottom.

Consider yourself warned!

There are certain surgical procedures that nobody likes to do. There are even procedures that people are afraid to be involved with. These are the surgeries where you could be exposed to diseases and unmentionably gross and disgusting things.

Personally speaking, I think rectal warts rank at the top of the list of things I'd rather not be involved with. Especially the extreme cases I've seen.

Let me give you a visual. Go to your supermarket and buy a medium sized head of cauliflower. Bend over and stick it between your butt cheeks. Please don't do this in the supermarket. I shouldn't have to say that, but then again... Now, keep it there for three or four months until it turns soft and gray and grows some hair.

Hey, I warned you!

I was new to surgery when I saw my first case of rectal warts. I was in the operating room, in my sterile gown and gloves waiting for the patient to be brought in when a nurse walked up to me and said, "You're going to need this."

She began smearing menthol ointment on my mask. The smell was over-powering. I asked her, "How come?"

Her eyes squinted and crows-feet appeared so I knew she was smiling under her mask. In a musical tone she said, "You'll see."

She opened up a sterile package and tossed a clear plastic tube onto my instrument table. The tube was large enough to accommodate your thumb. I glanced at the package the nurse had thrown in the garbage. The label read, *Smoke Evacuator*. In the same musical tone the nurse had used, I heard myself say, "Uh oh."

The doors to the operating room opened and an already anesthetized male patient was rolled into the room on a gurney. He was placed face down on the operating table with a sheet covering his back.

When the nurse pulled the sheet off, I involuntarily blurted, "God dam, what the fuck is that?"

The guy had a huge head of gray gooey cauliflower sticking out of his ass.

It was the grossest thing I'd ever seen in my life. I couldn't take my eyes off it.

I continued my uncontrollable blurting with, "Oh…My…God," periodically changing the emphasis on each word.

The surgeon backed into the room holding his wet hands up in front of him. I offered him a sterile towel and began saying, "Good morning Doctor."

He cut me off with a stern, "We're gonna make this quick."

I gowned and gloved the surgeon and his entourage of residents and medical students. None of them looked exceptionally happy to be there.

The patient was covered with sterile drapes and the suction tubing and electro-cautery machine was connected.

The surgeon looked at the anesthesiologist and asked, "Ok to cut?"

When he nodded his head, the surgeon immediately held up his hand and ordered, "Bovie!" I put it in his hand and he began cutting into and around the huge wart thing.

Let me stop here and explain what a 'Bovie' is. It's an electrosurgical device that applies high-frequency electric current to tissue. This enables the surgeon to cut, coagulate, desiccate and fulgurate tissue. If you don't have a medical dictionary handy, that's OK, it just means you can cut tissue without a lot of blood loss. Minimizing blood loss in surgery, as you can imagine, is very important.

What the surgeon holds in his hand looks like a plastic pencil and has a flat piece of metal at its tip that resembles a miniature butter knife. This pencil is attached by a wire to a box that generates the electrical current. Also attached to this machine is a grounding pad that's stuck to the patient.

You've heard horror stories of patients being burned and drapes catching on fire during operations? A poorly grounded electrosurgical unit is usually to blame. That, or the Anesthesiologist is sneaking a cigarette.

The term "bovie" is an informal name referring to its inventor, Dr. William T. Bovie. A Harvard man, circa 1926.

So there you have it. It's an amazing, indispensable piece of technology in modern-day surgery. Blah, blah, blah. That's the upside. The downside is that anytime you put electrical current to tissue with the intent of frying said tissue. It creates smoke.

Human tissue tends to put off quite a bit of smoke when you burn it. Rectal warts, on the other hand, put off incredible amounts of smoke.

As far as burning flesh goes, I consider rectal wart smoke to be one of the most toxic. Who knows what's floating around in that viral plume of smoke. All I know is that I don't want to breath it!

Enter, The Smoke Evacuator. "Ooooo." Under normal surgical conditions; let's say when you're cutting into someone's belly or just frying a bleeding vein, the normal suction apparatus will take care of things just fine.

But when you're talking Toxic Butt Smoke, you need to bring in the heavy artillery. You need an industrial grade; monster sucking, micron-filtering tube and you need as many as you can get your hands on. In the Navy this would be, "All hands on deck. Man your battle stations. This is not a drill."

On this particular cauliflower burning extraction bonfire, everyone with a free hand had a smoke evacuator suction tube and was frantically sucking up every molecular toxic trail of smoke the surgeon was creating.

Every stray wisp of smoke was accompanied by a chorus of, "Get it, get it, get it!" by the surgical team. I won't describe the actual removal of said grossness because it is just too disgusting. Mere words could never do justice to the ghastly image seared into my visual cortex. It's an olfactory image no amount of mentholated jelly smeared on my mask or post-op alcoholic binge can erase.

The way I deal with things like this is simple. I block it out. I psychologically screw myself up so bad and bury it so deep, a twelve hundred dollar an hour psychiatrist couldn't find it with a blowtorch.

What I choose to remember is how funny everyone looked dancing around, sucking and dodging mushroom clouds of smoke.

I have enormous respect for surgeons. They're a dedicated lot. I watched as his head disappeared in a rising blue-gray smoky haze.

I sucked until I could see his face and asked, "How do people get these?"

He almost laughed at me, "You gotta be kidding, right?"

I thought about it for a second, "Um, no, I'm not. They didn't spend a lot of time in school telling us about a huge head of cauliflower hanging off a guy's ass."

The Surgeon kept cutting away at the monstrosity, "You get these by sticking the wrong things up your ass!"

That made me ponder the question. Are there any "right things" to stick up your ass? I couldn't think of any off hand.

A masked head popped in the door of our operating room, then instantly disappeared. I heard the pitter-patter of running feet and someone yelling, "Butt smoke. Run, run for your life!"

This was my introduction to large rectal warts and how to remove them. I didn't eat cauliflower for years after this.

PUTTING A BETTER FACE ON THINGS

CHART TALK #2
Purloined Hospital Records

Just to prove that doctors are human and make mistakes like all the rest of us, we decided to show you some patient chart notes from actual medical records as dictated by physicians. Surely they could not all be transcription errors...

- By the time he was admitted, his rapid heart had stopped, and he was feeling better
- She has had no rigors or shaking chills, but her husband states she was very hot in bed last night.
- The patient has been depressed ever since she began seeing me in 1983.
- Patient was released to outpatient department without dressing.
- I have suggested that he loosen his pants before standing, and then, when he stands with the help of his wife, they should fall to the floor.
- The patient is tearful and crying constantly. She also appears to be depressed.
- Discharge status: Alive but without permission.
- The patient will need disposition, and therefore we will get Dr. Blank to dispose of him.
- Healthy appearing decrepit 69 year-old male, mentally alert but forgetful.
- The patient refused an autopsy.
- The patient has no past history of suicides.

- The patient expired on the floor uneventfully.
- Patient has left his white blood cells at another hospital.
- The patient's past medical history has been remarkably insignificant with only a 40 pound weight gain in the past three days.
- She slipped on the ice and apparently her legs went in separate directions in early December.
- The patient experienced sudden onset of severe shortness of breath with a picture of acute pulmonary edema at home while having sex which gradually deteriorated in the emergency room.
- The patient had waffles for breakfast and anorexia for lunch.
- Between you and me, we ought to be able to get this lady pregnant.
- The patient was in his usual state of good health until his airplane ran out of gas and crashed.
- Since she can't get pregnant with her husband, I thought you would like to work her up.
- While in the ER, she was examined, X-rated and sent home.
- The skin was moist and dry.
- Occasional, constant, infrequent headaches.
- Coming from Detroit, this man has no children.
- Patient was alert and unresponsive
- When she fainted, her eyes rolled around the room.

Goodbye Poop: A Child's Primer to a Healthy Colon

Richard Brown

(Inspired by my colonoscopy. Apologies to Margaret Wise Brown and "Goodnight Moon")

Hello laxative
Hello throne
Hello gurgling from my intestinal zone

Goodbye poop
Goodbye soup
Goodbye liquids in my digestive loop

Goodbye urine
Goodbye gas
Goodbye odors emanating from my ass

Goodbye corn
Goodbye beans
Goodbye tasty sources of proteins

Goodbye fish
Goodbye meat
Goodbye fiber in the form of wheat

Goodbye cookies
Goodbye chips
Goodbye chocolate that attaches to my hips

Goodbye yogurt
Goodbye juice
Goodbye stool that's exceedingly loose

Goodbye pizza
Goodbye zitis
Goodbye carbs flushed out in my feces

Goodbye soda
Goodbye beer
Hello "I'm still on the toilet, dear"

Hello IV
Hello gown
Hello camera about to be shoved uptown

Goodbye consciousness
Hello sleep
Goodbye procedure of which I won't hear a peep

Hello good news
Goodbye fears
Goodbye doctor for another five years

Getting Snippy
Pete Malicki

"Yes sir, I did hear it go off. The sirens of an incoming air raid are rather hard to miss. But like I said to you a moment ago when you asked me that very same question, I have no metal on me aside from the pins they put in my tibia after removing the tumor. Would you like me to take off my clothes to prove it to you?"

I could see the moron struggling to hold onto his professionalism and instantly regretted the question. He asked me to put the leg through first, which I managed to convince him would be impossible without the crutches he'd sent down to quarantine on account of their high wood content and possible risk to local biodiversity. I narrowly avoided a strip search but I did end up down to my underpants with a very suspicious Customs officer trying to work out how to ask permission to inspect my vagina for a hidden coin reel or whatever it was they thought was posing a risk to the safety of the airways. The pain in my abdomen was making it hard for me to retain my composure and I eventually left the airport to catch a taxi to the interstate bus terminal, where they don't care so much if you feel like blowing things up.

I phoned my husband. "I'm going to be late, dear. About sixteen hours. Sorry? In the cupboard by the living room entrance. Because they wouldn't let me on the plane, darling. What? Third shelf. Because they thought I had a grenade up my woo woo. Because that's the best place to hide a grenade. Huh? Third shelf from the top *or* the bottom, darling. The shelf happens to be in the middle. Because that's where we've always kept the bloody toilet paper. If you'd changed it before in your life, you might know that. And I'm not entirely sure what you've been wiping your bum with these last few days. Anyway, it's an overnight coach and I'll be back tomorrow morning, if you could pick me up from the terminal in the city. No I don't eat it; I'm a woman. We use more of it than you. Pardon? Because I just had multiple surgeries and the pain is twenty times worse than the damned hernia, darling, and I don't fancy taking my chances on the tram. If you're not there tomorrow I will divorce you. Have a lovely evening."

The bus ride home would have been quite instructive to the secret service. After three hours of a teenage girl's phone conversation, eight hours of cacophonous snoring, another two hours of the teenager, a moment of silence filled with the smell of tuna fish and what I swear was rotting cabbage—all punctuated by three screaming babies and an old man's flatulence—I was ready to divulge my nation's most precious secrets just to make it all stop. I distracted myself with images of my husband having to shower every time he did a number two on account of his inability to find the toilet paper. I focused on the agonising pain in my gut just to keep my sanity.

I'd been what you call a "surgery tourist." We aren't exactly poor, but my husband doesn't earn the greatest salary on account of his stupidity and I'm an overworked, underpaid school teacher. When a hospital several thousand miles away offers not only a package deal on hernia operations and cancerous tumour removals but an additional seventy percent off, people like me take the deal without asking questions. I'm beginning to regret not asking, "Are you sure this isn't overnight surgery?" I felt a little like I'd been rushed out of there before I was ready to leave the painkillers behind.

The bus finally arrived and I dragged my exhausted ass out onto the street, where I expected to find my husband waiting grumpily. At first I thought he wasn't there, but he came out of a nearby café before the call to my lawyer connected. He had thoughtfully purchased three delicious things my recent abdominal surgery prevented me from consuming but I did genuinely appreciate the sentiment. I climbed into the front passenger seat and was asleep before he'd even started the engine.

We arrived home and I stumbled past the pile of discarded knickknacks near the cupboard and collapsed on my bed. Surgery and insomnia had kicked my butt and I slept for twelve hours straight, only waking once when my husband turned in. When I woke up early the next morning, I discovered something very interesting. I couldn't move. Not an inch.

"Honey?" I managed between gritted teeth. "Could you kindly phone an ambulance? I think the alien eggs in my intestines have just hatched."

I woke my husband by blowing in his ear, which was about all I could physically manage, and repeated the comment. His sympathy valve doesn't start working until midday so he rather grudgingly climbed out of the warmth of the bed and headed downstairs to call the emergency services. I'm fairly certain he stopped for breakfast on the way because it was a full five minutes before I heard him call out, "What's wrong with you exactly?"

"I had surgery yesterday," I said, trying to shout but finding it too painful to go above a four-out-of-ten in the volume department.

"What?" he called back. "Speak up, will you."

I prayed silently for his death. His head appeared in the doorway a moment later and his exasperated expression only made me want to kill him harder. Fortunately, I passed out when I tried to throw my

Ludlum at him and woke up being bundled downstairs on a stretcher by a pair of paramedics. The next twenty minutes passed in a semiconscious haze and it wasn't until I'd reached the hospital and been pumped full of pethidine that I could focus on what was happening.

"Mrs. Warden. Can you tell me where it hurts?"

A doctor about half my age was standing beside me wearing a very professional look of concern. My face had gone slack; the painkillers had taken my muscle tone.

"Everywhere," I mumbled. He asked me to be more specific and I said, "everywhere that's a part of my body." This didn't satisfy him so he began prodding me and asking me to rate my pain out of ten. How does one do that? Is ten out of ten "wonderful pain?"

Long story short, it hurt a lot more—surprise, surprise—around my abdomen, where I'd had the hernia fixed. He palpated me and frowned.

"Mrs. Warden, you didn't have a perforated intestine did you? Or a muscle tear? I feel an unusual lump right here."

I already knew what it was. "They left a pair of surgical scissors inside of me, didn't they?"

"No, that's simply impossible. Ever since someone left a pair inside that French woman, fool proof checks and balances have been implemented in hospitals around the world."

Never underestimate how expert some fools are.

"Could you be a dear and run me through an X-ray all the same?"

"That's really not necessary. There must be a more reasonable explanation."

After a considerable amount of back and forth between myself, the young doctor and numerous other hospital staff, I got my X-ray and they did indeed find a pair of snippers in my abdomen. I was beginning to see why the discount was so generous: discount on price, discount on quality.

Some head surgeon or other came to see me. "Mrs. Warden, this is the first time we've seen this not only in this hospital but in this entire *country*."

I marvelled at my uniqueness.

"We're going to need to pop you open and fetch these scissors back for you. I'm sure the good folk at St. Mercy Discount Hospital will be wanting them back."

"Oh yes," I retorted, "better send them via Express Post before I get charged with theft."

"Now, now, Mrs. Warden. There's no need to get snippy with me. Tell me, do you have health insurance?"

"I can't afford it, I'm afraid. Why? You're not saying I have to pay to have these removed? Surely you can send the damned bill to Mercy on account of their medical malpractice and all."

"The sad fact of the matter, Mrs. Warden, is that that's between you and St. Mercy. If we operate on you, it uses our precious resources, and we simply cannot afford to do so if we're not getting reimbursed. I'm sure you'll sue them quite successfully and make yourself a pretty profit."

I was flummoxed. "How much will this operation cost me?"

"Eight thousand dollars, including third party surgical mishap insurance."

"Surgical mishap insurance? Is that... oh look, don't worry about it. I'll go home and watch the tele for a few weeks before I expire. Enjoy having my inevitable death on your conscience, doctor."

The head surgeon put his hand on my knee and leaned in close. "Mrs. Warden, you realise St. Mercy would do it for free?"

"You realise that's a sixteen hour drive from here!"

"I'll pay for you to call a cab."

"You'll pay for the cab or the phone call?"

"The phone call."

"I'd like you to leave now."

"I understand. Good luck, Mrs. Warden."

The surgeon left the room and I lay back, tears coming into my eyes as I stared a hole in the ceiling. I couldn't cope with the bus ride back to St Mercy Discount Hospital. I simply couldn't. It would be roughly as tolerable as if I were to cut open my own abdomen and pull the damned scissors out myself.

Actually, that wasn't such a bad idea. When they found my mangled body on their premises they'd have no choice but to fix me and I could pay the bill after I got my money out of St. Mercy.

No, I had an even better idea!

I climbed off the bed, clenching my jaw hard to stop me from screaming with agony. Dragging myself over to some shelving, I opened a few packets of surgical instruments and scattered them strategically around the floor. A nurse came into the room *just* as I was sitting back down on the edge of the bed.

"Should you be getting up, Mrs Warden?" he asked. "Why don't you lay back down?"

"No, I just need to…"

I stepped on a scalpel and my foot slipped out from underneath me. I landed heavily on the floor. I landed heavily *on a pair of surgical scissors* on the floor. They perforated my intestines. The witness… I mean nurse…

rushed over and lifted me back onto the bed before running off to fetch some doctors.

Many months later, the colostomy bag had been retired permanently and I sat sipping cocktails by the pool. Both medical malpractice lawsuits had gone my way and I was now a multimillionaire, every day marvelling at the wonderful nature of the society we'd built around ourselves. It was a trying time when we had nothing coming in but lawyers' fees; my husband tried to leave me so I promised him a couple of Porsches and he stuck it through to the end. It was a good result.

Aside from the money, I ended up with a gut covered in scars and a very important life lesson.

Well, to be honest, there were actually about a dozen life lessons, all of them as important as the last.

But I'll let you work them out yourselves.

I have to fetch another piña colada.

A doctor has a stethoscope up to a man's chest. The man asks "Doc, how do I stand?" The doctor says "That's what puzzles me!"
Henny Youngman

When Make-a-Wish Goes Bad
Dan McQuinn

–Mommy, this isn't the usual route to the hospital.

–We're not going to the hospital today.

–But what about my treatments?

–Dr. Robinson said it would be OK if you miss one day.

–But where are we going?

–You'll see.

–Hey, there's the stadium where the Colts play. Why are you pulling in the parking lot? There's no game today.

–I said you'll see.

–There's some of the Colts holding a sign and balloons. Is that Peyton Manning?

–It sure is.

–"Welcome Tommy" … All of this is for me?

–That's right. It's a Make-a-Wish. Are you surprised?

–Oh my fucking God! I knew it. I'm fucking dying!

With Luv, to Bob, Kate, and the Surgeon
Saralee Perel

When I have just one sip of alcohol, I tell mere acquaintances that I love them. So you can imagine what I'm like under anesthesia. Last month I had an operation. Everything, thank God, turned out fine. But I was a nervous wreck.

As the operating team swarmed around me, I pleaded, "I need a lot of anesthesia – I mean A LOT!" Kate was my anesthesiologist. I grabbed her arm. "I mean . . ." She started the IV sedation. "I mean, I mean . . . AH LUV YOUUU . . ."

I had a growth in my uterus that had to be removed. My surgeon came over and asked if I had questions. I looked at him through unfocused eyes, "Do you LUV me?" I slurred.

The hospital is a teaching hospital. The surgeon asked my permission to take pictures for his students. "You are a very, very sick man," I said.

"They won't show your face," he said.

"Oh that's even better, you freak."

I felt searing pain when they began. "OW! I'm dying here! He's cutting me open! I need some real strong pain medication! He's killing me!"

"He hasn't started yet," Kate said.

"Oh." I fell asleep. A few minutes later I woke up and touched Kate's arm. "You are my very best friend in the whole entire world. I LUV you."

Later, in the recovery area, I was thrilled to see my husband, Bob. I held up my arms, in slow motion, for a hug. We held each other tight. "The doctor told me you were fine and he showed me the pictures," he said.

"Did he get my good side?"

"You don't understand. These were medical pictures."

"Right. You know they'll be in the National Enquirer next month."

Then I had a mid-life hot flash. Lying on the gurney, I grabbed the bottom hem of my hospital johnnie. I pulled it up to my forehead to wipe away the sweat, leaving me totally naked. Bob grabbed the johnnie and quickly pulled it back down over me.

"I'm hot!" I said, pulling the johnnie back up to my forehead.

"Everyone can see you!" he said, covering me back up.

"So what?" I said, still under the effects of anesthesia, "What do you think they've been doing for the last hour? Looking up my nose?"

He firmly held the gown below my knees, smiling uncomfortably at everyone.

"Yoo hooo!" I waved to my nurse. "I'm ready to go home now."

She came over. "Can you walk?"

"Can I walk? Watch this." I rolled to the side of the gurney. I forgot to stop rolling. I hit the floor.

I've learned a lot from this experience. Primarily about perspective. If I have a cold, it doesn't matter. If my truck breaks down, it doesn't matter. If a repair-person doesn't show up, well – that still drives me nuts.

But now I worry about what's next. I suppose there's always going to be a "what's next." I have a pompous acquaintance who's a psychiatrist. In place of each numeral on his watch is the word, "NOW." When I first saw that, I wanted to puke. And when I think about it today, I still do. But he's basically right. So until the next thing hits, I'm luxuriating as much as I can in the "now." I don't want to miss any of the good stuff right in front of me, by worrying about things that haven't happened yet.

Secondly, I will tell my best pal, Bob, that I LUV him. I'll say it often. After all, we never know what's next. Other than, "It's benign," what better words are there to hear?

A woman visits her clinic and spends some time sitting in the waiting room. Just as she's starting to wonder when she'll be seen, a large black retriever enters the room, wagging its tail. It comes over to her, licks her hand and leg, sniffs her crotch, then pads out of the room.

Before she can figure out what to think about that, a beautiful Siamese cat strides haughtily into the room and jumps up on the chair beside her. It sits there, solemnly regarding her from head to foot, sniffs around her in a condescending manner, meows arrogantly, and slithers out of the room.

She shakes her head and continues to wait until a medical secretary comes in holding some papers. She thinks she's finally being seen and stands, but the secretary says, "Okay, here's your bill. Who's your insurance carrier?"

Flabbergasted, she asks, "Bill for *what*? I've been here an hour and haven't even been seen!"

Putting on her glasses to scan the paperwork, the secretary shakes her head and points to the billing numbers. "No, it says right here you had Lab tests and a CAT scan."

Living with Glaucoma: What to Expect from your First Marijuana Treatment

Ben Link

After consuming your marijuana or other THC-laced product, find a comfortable seat in your residence. It may take some time before you notice the effects, so find an activity to pass the time. Maybe you could watch a movie? Better scroll through Netflix to see what's streaming. Remember, THC releases a flood of serotonin into the brain, which will cause feelings of joy, happiness and/or euphoria. A comedy may be an appropriate choice for entertainment, but that new Terrence Malick movie might blow your mind. Whatever you decide, make sure you keep your laptop nearby just in case you need to look up anything on IMDB. The last thing you want is to waste 30 minutes trying to figure out if it was Justin Long who made that cameo or if it was some new actor you've never heard of who just looks like Justin Long.

Eventually you will experience a numbness in the front of your forehead. The fluid pressure in your eyes will begin to alleviate. That's the THC taking a hold and easing your glaucoma pains. You may even regain some vision, which would be pretty sweet. Now don't you feel good? I mean, who would have thought it'd be this easy? After all, you deserve to feel better. Just because you manage your glaucoma by alternative means doesn't make you a criminal or anything. Can't they see you're a kind-hearted, contributing member of society? There's no reason to arrest people for possessing marijuana when so many are living in pain. This is bullshit! Those lawmakers are probably paid off by the pharmaceutical companies, so they can rake in more profits from their "legal" drug sales.

Oh shit! Don't forget to take your prescription meds if you haven't already done so. As much as you don't like them, they do help you feel better. Plus if you take them now then all those side effects you hate will be relieved by the marijuana. There's, some sort of canceling effect where the marijuana turns off, or maybe turns on, the brain's receptors, which your pills normally use to make you puke. Well, guess what? That ain't gonna happen when you're high as balls! Marijuana will swoop in there and be like "You can't make him sick!" (Waving its finger in the air) "If you wanna make him sick, then you gotta get through me! This is my house! And you're not welcome in *my* house!" Then the side effects will run away, and you and marijuana can high five and go on a fun adventure.

Speaking of adventures, now's a good time to see if you have anything to eat in the kitchen. You could order delivery, but why risk having to explain yourself to the delivery person? It'd be like, "Yes, I'm high, but no it's not because I'm bored. I have glaucoma. This is how I treat my disease, thank you very much. Now give me that pizza. Sixteen bucks, right? Let's see what's in the 'ol wallet here. All I have are twenties. You have change? Umm, give me back two? Yeah, two dollars is fine. Wait. Is that a good tip? I don't know. What's normal? Oh forget it. Keep it all. No, never mind. I'll take the two dollars. OK, thanks, man. See you later." Or something to that extent.

Anyways if you're still on the couch thinking, go ahead and make your way to the kitchen now. Who cares if you've never cooked before? That won't stop you from creating the most delicious meal ever! Marijuana has been shown to make users more creative. Since you smoked some really good bud, that makes you extra creative. Feel free to open cabinets you hardly use, grab a wok or something crazy like that, and fix something so ridiculous you'll have mouth orgasms. Put a bunch of leftovers in a flour tortilla and squirt some hot sauce all over it. Whatever spices you can find, add those, too. Your goal is to create a flavor explosion that'll make you forget you ever had glaucoma! And don't forget to have something sweet on the side, like Gushers. Oh, man! Do you have any Gushers? Look around for some Gushers. That'd be amazing if you had Xtreme Kiwi Xplosion flavored ones. God, they'd probably cure your glaucoma if you ate them right now.

With your belly now full and the marijuana's effects waning, it's time to strategize a sleep plan. One option is to return to the couch, grab a blanket and surround yourself with pillows (lots of pillows). Another option is your bed. If you can make it to your bed, that'd be the ultimate. It's no secret you want to sleep there, but the couch has been good to you so far. Why ruin a good thing? Of course, you could grab the pillows and covers from your bed and sleep on the couch. Then you'd have the best of both worlds. Then again, that could be a lot of work with little pay off. Go for the bed. It was built with sleeping people in mind.

Quickly run and jump into your bed as fast as you can. It'll be cold at first. Feel free to scream a little bit while you wiggle around under the covers. This'll get your heart rate up, and the friction will make the bed warmer faster. Once you've formed a comfortable cocoon, take a deep breath. Your glaucoma should be nothing but an afterthought. You have successfully completed your first marijuana treatment. Don't forget: as long as you can buy a fat sack, you will be totally fine. The only thing that could go wrong is if your dealer gets arrested or moves out of the city or, even worse, raises his prices. But don't think about that. It'll give you nightmares.

Now go to sleep and dream about working in a futuristic city where you're a time cop. Goodnight.

You Know You've Joined a Redneck HMO if:

- The annual breast exam is conducted at Hooter's

- Directions to the Doctor's office include: "Take a left when you enter the trailer park"

- The tongue depressors taste faintly of Fudgesicles

- The only proctologist lists his address as Rotorooter

- The Lone Star Bar and Grill is an approved pharmacy

- Your primary care physician is wearing the pants you gave to Goodwill last month

- Preventive Care Coverage includes "an apple a day"

- Your Prozac comes in colors and has little "M's" on each pill

- The only 100% covered expense is embalming

- Your Viagra prescription includes a popsicle stick and some duct tape

First Response Heroes
Public Domain

Actual answers given by students on pre-med exams around the world.

General:

"The body consists of three parts - the brainium, the borax, and the abominable cavity. The brainium contains the brain; the borax, the heart and lungs; and the abominable cavity, the bowls, of which there are five - a, e, i, o, and u."

Respiration:

"When you breathe, you inspire. When you do not breathe, you expire"
"Respiration consists of two acts: first inspiration, then expectoration."

Cardiovascular:

"The three kinds of blood vessels are arteries, veins, and caterpillars."

Gastrointestinal:

"The alimentary canal is located in the northern part of Alabama."

Orthopaedics:

"The skeleton is what is left after the insides have been taken out and the outsides have been taken off. The purpose of the skeleton is something to hitch meat on."

Dentistry:
"A permanent set of teeth consists of eight canines, eight cuspids, two molars, and eight cuspidors."

Reproductive medicine:
"Artificial insemination is when the farmer does it to the cow instead of the bull."

"To prevent contraception, wear a condominium."

"Many women believe that an alcoholic binge will have no effects on the unborn fetus, but that is a large misconception."

Hematology:
"Before giving a blood transfusion, find out if the blood is affirmative or negative."

Eyes and nose:
"To remove dust from the eye: pull the eye down over the nose."

"For nosebleeds, put the nose lower than the body until the heart stops."

"For a cold: use an agoniser to spray the nose until it drops in your throat."

First aid:
"For fainting: rub the person's chest or, if a lady, rub her arm above the head instead. Or put the head between the knees of the nearest doctor."

"For asphyxiation: apply artificial respiration until the patient is dead."

"For drowning: climb on top of the person and move up and down to make artificial perspiration."

"For dog bite: put the dog away for several days. If he has not recovered, then kill it."

The Ma'ams-O-Gram
Cindy Brown

It's that time of year again. The time of year women love to hate.

It's time... for the yearly check-ups. You ladies know the ones I'm talking about. I'm talking about getting poked, felt up, internally scraped while a duck-bill holds your hoo-ha open, and getting your boobs smashed. Yes, it's female check-up time.

The pap. The mammogram. The *horror*.

A lot of women call their breasts, "The girls" and I like that term. I think I first heard it used by Stacy London on What Not to Wear. I'm thinking at this stage in life, however, my girls have become "The ma'ams." I'm no spring chicken anymore and I hate being called ma'am, but really it is more fitting.

Let's just say that you're walking down the street with a nice shirt accentuating the positives. Would you be comfortable with a man ogling your "girls"? The term "girls" makes me think of my daughters, so this makes me feel just a tad bit uncomfortable.

Now, think about the same situation and as you pass a fellow sporting a nice gray suit walking down the street, he acknowledges your bosom with a nice tip of his hat and, addressing each boob separately, he smiles and says to the left one, "Hello, ma'am," then looks respectively toward the right, but doesn't look directly at it and says, "and good day to you also ma'am!" This is of course unrealistic, so let's just say that he then leaps onto a lamp-post and dances on down the street singing a song about beautiful women like a Fred Astaire movie, while glancing back at you adoringly. Pfft. Fantasies. They're so crazy!

So, first on my agenda this year is the mammogram, or as I now call it, the "ma'ams-o-gram." I've only been forced to endure this torture for a few years now and I have to say that I don't like it. I don't like it one bit. First of all, you have to go topless in front of strangers. If you've already gone to the gyno for the other check-up, then you've already been felt up by the doctor, now you have to expose yourself to a stranger and get your boob smashed in a vise. This does not equal fun in my book.

Also, I've talked about the boob thing recently. They're big. It hurts! And for those of you who haven't gone through this yet, do you know what they tell you as they're smashing it in the vise to get the images? "Tell me when you can't stand it anymore." They mean *the pain.* I honestly wonder if a boob has ever exploded on them because somebody had a high pain tolerance and forgot to cry "uncle."

Not only are you half naked with a stranger and getting your boob mercilessly flattened like a panini, just at the moment you're about to pass out from the pain, they tell you this: "Now lift up your chin as high as you can." If foreign countries aren't using this as a torture method, they really should be.

Imagine me, humor writer, with the boob in the vise, in pain, and then instructed to look up, thus increasing the already searing pain to eleven. Yes, the pain goes to eleven. I envisioned in my mind what I must have looked like and thought about what a funny picture it would be for my blog and I busted out laughing right when she was taking the picture. Sure enough, it was blurry and she had to do it AGAIN! Oh Lord, what had I done? Curse you, sense of humor!

As if that wasn't bad enough, there was a wrinkle in the first boob picture, which had gone swimmingly, and she had to do that one again, too! Are you seeing where the word "horrors" came in? Fellas, do they have *ANY* sort of test where they smash your winkie flat? I didn't think so. If there is such a test, please alert me so that I can become a technician.

"What do you do for a living?"

"I smash wankers, that's what I do. And I love my job."

Now, at least my ma'ams-o-gram wasn't lengthy, I thought, and I was in and out of there in a half an hour flat. "You'll get a paper in the mail next week," they proclaimed. I took my free gift (a manicure set and two Hershey's kisses, only one of which was eaten upon arrival at home that night by a child; I knew I should have eaten them in the car... "My boobs got smashed, those are MY chocolates!") and I was on my way.

So yesterday morning when the phone rang and I saw who it was on the caller ID, I knew it wasn't good news. Sure enough, they need to take another look because they "saw something, which could be nothing at all, but we need some more views" and then they might send me to the hospital for an ultrasound right after if it still looks suspicious after the doc looks at the images.

She was a lovely woman on the phone and did her best to encourage me that it could be nothing, could be just a fluid-filled cyst, etc. but of course you know from past posts that what I heard was that it could be just a tiny little skull and crossbones we need to address. Fred Astaire, where are you now to sing and dance for me?

I assured her that she was talking to the right person and that no matter what it is, I will find a way to laugh about it and that I will probably blog about it too. And of course, I am.

So my follow-up is tomorrow. I've had many women tell me "Oh, I had that happen too and turned out to be nothing." However, I am realistically looking at the fact that I know two women in stage 4 breast cancer as well. Plus they never came up with any result on my throat problem. What I thought were ENT troubles gave the doc no concern, but other symptoms like the choking and voice change did, so she ran bloodwork and I had a thyroid ultrasound done, which both came back fine.

Thought for the day: I'm either dying of throat-breast cancer or I'm fine, either one. No matter. I'm going to keep on living my life and writing until the day I die. I know it can be done because I actually followed someone who did that very thing. Such respect I have for her. She died of the same rare breast cancer my aunt has.

You know what they say, no pain, no gain! In all seriousness, go get that ma'ams-o-gram, ladies! It could very well save your life and that is worth all the discomfort.

My doctor is wonderful. Once, in 1955, when I couldn't afford an operation, he touched up the X-rays.
Joey Bishop

Ma'ams-O-Gram: Take Two with a Twist
Cindy Brown

I cannot promise this will be my last post about boobs, but honestly I'm about to declare May 2012 as "Boob Month" on my blog. I thought this post would be the last one about boobs, but then I saw the controversial Time magazine cover and I might have to talk about that in the next post, I'm not sure yet. I'd be interested in hearing your opinions more than giving my own and I'm sure it's a hot topic in the blogosphere.

Now, back to my boobs! I went for my follow up and I have to say that I was pretty worried. This time, they put me in a special consultation room with a reclining chair for me to undress and wait and I immediately thought that meant they were most likely making me comfortable for the inevitable bad news. Then a lady who looked like she held an important position came in and told me not to be concerned if they did send me for the ultrasound after the new images, that it still would just be precautionary. I was sure I would be going. I was worried.

Being the sheeple (I read that term for religious people the other day and I love it) that I am, I of course thought that I should say a little prayer in my head before the "photo shoot" (another term I read today and love, thank you Cheryl) and that's when it got weird and I sent myself into another laugh attack. I cannot believe the idiotic prayer my brain chose.

It went like this: "In the name of Jesus, I just give this test to you today and I put my breast in your hands..."

Then it hit me. I busted out laughing. Oh my God, I just asked Jesus to grab my boob. I couldn't even finish the prayer because I couldn't stop giggling. I hadn't said it purposely that way in my head, but again, curse my sense of humor! That's how it came out without even thinking! How could I have possibly worded that prayer any worse? Then my mind went crazy.

Would God see the humor in my prayer? I hoped so. Or am I just headed straight for the fiery dungeons because my mind works that way? We're made in His image, right? So He's gotta have an awesome sense of humor. Don't be mad, Jesus. I didn't really mean to ask you to grab my boob!

I imagined Jesus hearing my prayer and doubling over with laughter, then straightening, facing his Father, and saying, "Can I, Dad? You did a great job on that pair." Then Jesus would laugh hysterically while saying, "I'm just messin' with ya! Oh, I crack myself up! Grab her boob! Like I would do that! Ha ha ha haahhahahaaha!" while God gives Jesus a "Don't you even think about it" stare and taps his toe in disapproval.

"Young Deity, go to your room!"
"Gosh, Dad, I was only kidding, gah!"
"Don't take my name in vain, young man!"
"I didn't, I just said, 'gah,' - I didn't mean you!"
"Don't give me any lip, young man."
"Jeez, Dad..."
"And don't take your own name in vain either!"

Somebody's probably really going to hate this post. I almost named it, "Jesus, Please Hold This Boob." Hey, I'm a Christian, but I am as real as they get. Deal with it, or go read another blog. Your hate mail will be "returned to sender".

Thankfully, I composed myself before the tech came to get me. I was relieved that it was only one breast this

116

time. She positioned me and then funny part number two happened. She said, "Okay, now I'm going to have to just twist your breast for these just a little bit."

Great, she's literally giving me a titty-twister. Fellas, I know that even you have had a titty-twister at some point around fourth grade, but Lord Almighty, when they're squashing it AND simultaneously twisting it, crap-a-tootie! Finally, she finished and I went back for "the wait" while the radiologist looked at the images. I got to freak out again when she came back and announced "He said we need some more views using another paddle."

Great. *This* paddle has a circular thing that looks like the underside of a cup holder that isolates the area better. Then she got out a ruler and started taking measurements! I giggled again, thinking, "Okay, I know they're big, but really... it's no Guinness World Record or anything." I decided to keep that joke to myself. I didn't want to laugh because she was trying to be precise in pinpointing the area of concern and I didn't want more images and thus, *more pain*. Still, it seemed like she was making blueprints out of my boob measurements. Weird.

After a second long wait in the reclining chair, my reading of National Geographic was interrupted with word that all was well and I should come back in a year. I said, "What! I went through all that for it to be nothing?" She informed me that was a good thing. Everyone keeps asking me what it was and I don't have the slightest idea. All I know is that it's not of concern and really that's all I need to know right now. My concern is to figure out how to pay my 20% for the second mammo, radiologist, blah, blah, blah bills.

Whatever it was, I put it in Jesus' hands and it turned out okay after all, so I guess he did appreciate my sense of humor.

Prescription 4 Laffs
Connie Sedona

ETIOLOGY The study of pigging out.
ELECTROLYTE IMBALANCE When too many bulbs have burned out.
DUODENUM Jeans for Siamese twins.
HEMOCCULT The satanic worship of men.
HEMAQUIT Deprogram from hemoccult.
HIDASCAN Game played by x-ray techs.
MUSCLE ARTIFACT Arnold Schwarzenegger fossilized.
DISCHARGE Costing more or less dan dat charge.
CLAUSTROPHOBIA Abnormal fear of Santa.
ANTABUSE Report your uncle immediately!
ACYCLOVIR Swerving to avoid hitting another bike.
EUTHANASIA Chinese children.
URINATION The USA.
APONEUROSIS Fear of being on top.
SYNCOPE What you might get if your toilet backs up.
BENIGN What you want to be when you're eight.
PHOTIC STIMULATION Pornography.
IDIOTYPE What some doctors think transcriptionists do.
TESTICLE Experimenting with a feather.
ABRADE Hair style.
SEROUS Not kidding.
SENILE View Egyptian river.
SELDINGER Get rid of bell.
PERCUSSION THERAPY Repair work on drums.
SALPINX She blushes.
CARUNCLE Father's brother in auto business.
FURUNCLE Other brother who raises chinchillas.
FUNDUS Send money.
PROTIME No amateurs.
ANALLY Occurring yearly.

TUMOR An extra pair.

ARTERY The study of fine paintings.

TERMINAL ILLNESS Getting sick at the airport.

BACTERIA Back door to cafeteria.

SEROLOGY StudyofKnighthood.

BARIUM WhatyoudowhenCPRfails.

CESAREAN SECTION A district in Rome.

PROTEIN Favoring adolescents.

CATARRH A stringed musical instrument.

SECRETION Hiding anything.

D&C Where Washington is.

PAP SMEAR Fatherhood test.

NITRATE Cheaperthandayrate.

RECOVERY ROOM Place to do upholstery.

CAUTERIZE Made eye contact with her.

RECTUM Damn near killed 'em.

G.I. SERIES Ball games between soldiers.

POSTOPERATIVE Letter carrier.

DILATE To live long.

FIBULA A small lie.

GENITAL Non-Jewish.

DIARRHEA Journal of daily events.

IMPOTENT Distinguished, well known.

MEDICALSTAFF Doctor's cane.

LABOR PAIN Getting hurt at work.

LEVODOPA Italian for "Get a divorce."

MORBID Higher offer.

NODE Was aware of.

OUTPATIENT Person who has fainted.

ENEMA Not a friend.

- He was complaining of pain in the abdomen after stabbing himself with a pair of small sisters.

- There is a transverse laceration just proximal to the proximal wrist crease which is oblique and oriented proximally with a proximal skin flap.
- She had chickenpops, munks and measles as a child.
- Aggressive treatment was discontinued, and the patient succame to his widespread disease.
- "Our loved ones never seem to die when we want them to."
- The patient was having some chest pain radiating to her left arm.
- She had been using the plumber yesterday quite vigorously.
- She says the episodes are a bit more likely to happen when she is under stress or in heat.
- Apparently he has nymph load involvement.
- Before I started treating the patient he had a period of relative stability.
- She gets up once or twice a year.
- She was assessed roughly every 30 minutes.
- Patient has dentures upstairs.
- Left foot is slightly smaller than his wife.
- Patient addicted to young women …
- She does not smoke and has never smoken.
- ER note: The pelvic exam will be done later on the floor.
- He noted atypical chest pain in his throat.
- Rectal exam was deferred, as it is close to meal time.
- He is to keep the penis elevated.
- She was quite exhausted, having painted the house with her husband.

- The patient gets fatigued walking one block; on the other hand, she can shop all day.
- Apparently she was asymptomatic during her episodes of symptoms.
- She has three children, probably one of whom is socially acceptable.
- She had the onset of pain in January, at which time the pain started.
- He has had varicose brain surgery.
- The patient did receive blood during his transfusion
- The patient had mental fragments removed from his forehead after an auto accident.
- She lives in Palm Springs and plays golf, although she is nearly blind – a situation which probably improves her game.
- The patient takes Tegretol for pain given her by her neurologist.
- Bowel sounds were pleasant.
- The patient lives with her husband of many ears in Santa Rosa.
- The patient is getting better and starting to feel himself again.
- History was given by her husband who does not seem to be very familiar with the patient.
- She is married and has two brown children.
- Aggressively growling glioma.
- The patient is not thought to be an eminent treat to himself or his wife.
- Initially she was treated with oral gents.
- He required removal of a foreign boy from the lateral foot.

The Power of Suggestion
By Ernie Witham

There's a funny line in the movie City Slickers when Daniel Stern, during a tirade of complaints to Billy Crystal and Bruno Kirby about life on the open trail herding cattle, ends with something like: "...and I've got this rash!"

This thought came to me as I was sitting in the waiting area in the dermatology department at the clinic. There were a number of other people sitting there looking uncomfortable and I'm sure, like me, wanting to throw down their magazines, whip off some clothing and scratch like an old coon dog. But of course that's a no-no. With the power of suggestion one scratch could lead to a free-for-all and in no time we could end up with a small mountain of flaked off skin parts. Then maintenance would have to be called and it would be so loud with that industrial vacuum cleaner going that we might not hear our names called and be here for hours.

Speaking of suggestion, I've heard that during the Hippie years when LSD was popular there were certain things you did not do to someone who was tripping. For instance, you didn't say: "Wow, what's that awful smell?" Or: "Did you see the size of that rat that just scurried under your chair?" Or: "Wow, man, what's wrong with your face?" Other things you didn't do included yawning excessively, constantly clearing your throat and, of course, scratching relentlessly. Because once you started any of these things, the power of suggestion took over and no one could stop. To this day some old Hippies still have flashbacks... excuse me (yaaawwwnnnn, a-a-a-hem, yaaawwwnnnn, a-a-a-hem, yaaawwwnnnn, a-a-a-hem).

Today's clinic experience actually started in the crowded elevator. Because I can't stand the deafening silence of anonymity, I asked the guy next to me: "So what are you in for?"

"Colonoscopy," he whispered.

"First time?"

"Yes."

Others in the elevator nodded knowingly.

"It's not bad if you don't twitch."

"Yes," a women said, "best not to move suddenly when that probe is… probing."

The guy twitched a bit and a look of panic crept across his face.

"Um bummer, man," another guy said under his breath.

He twitched again. And again. And again.

I quickly changed the subject to ease his mind. "The good thing is between not eating for twenty-four hours and that stuff they make you drink the night before you usually loose a few pounds."

"I thought you drank the stuff in the morning?" the guy squeaked out.

"What?"

"Oh my."

"That's cutting it close."

This caused an animated discussion about the myriad of problems associated with not being completely ready for the procedure. When the elevator stopped, the guy rushed out and ran twitchingly toward the restroom.

"Good luck," we yelled after him.

"Hope he gets a doctor with a sense of humor."

"No kidding."

A lab technician got on the elevator. I asked her: "So, see anything unusual today?"

"Well," she said. The others leaned in closer. "We removed a wart from a kid's hand that looked a little like Harry Potter."

"Do you still have it?"

"I wish, but no, the kid wanted to keep it for show and tell."

"Did you at least get a picture of it?"

She pulled out here cell phone. "Wow," we all said.

"The strange thing is that it just popped up overnight and it's the fourth one we've seen this month. There seems to be a bit of a wart epidemic going around." Instantly, we all began checking our digits. I thought sure I felt a small bump on my left thumb.

The elevator stopped again and she got off. "Anyone for dermatology?" A guy held the door.

"Ah, me," I said.

"Remember," they said, "scratching only makes it worse. No matter how bad it itches, you should avoid scratching."

So that's what I was doing. Sitting in the dermatology waiting room not scratching. Thinking positive thoughts like how great it would be to jump into an ocean filled with ointment then lay on a blanket covered in anti-itch cooling gel.

"Mr. Witham? This way please."

I started to follow her toward one of the small exam rooms then I stopped, lifted my right arm, and scratched like crazy. It was pure mayhem as the door closed behind me.

Inside Medical Humor
Various Newspapers and Journals

From a leaflet on Sexually Transmitted Diseases
"We don't know why, but it seems that men don't get
bacterial vaginosis."

An apology that appeared recently in The Safety And
Health Practitioner
SORRY. We would like to apologize to readers for the late
arrival of our March issue, which was entitled 'Flammable
Materials : Controlling the Hazard!' The delay was caused
by a fire at the printers.

Advert in the British Journal of Medicine
FOR SALE : Real bone half-skeleton, in better condition
than seller. £250.

Seen in the BBC canteen in Manchester
In the interests of hygiene, please use tongues when
picking up your baked potatoes.

From an article on stomach trouble :-
'Doctors are beginning to accept that stomach ulcers are
infectious. They are caused by a bug called Helicopter'.

From More!
'Your chance of catching an STD during your period is
greater, because the blood changes the PhD level in the
vagina'.

The Sunday Times explanation for the extinction of the
dinosaurs : 'The extinction may well have occurred when a
steroid hit the Earth'.

Another Newspaper Misprint : 'The Welsh international
had to withdraw when the cut turned sceptic'.

From a Sunday Newspaper
'The surgeon said he'd removed my momentum - the funny apron of fat that covers the intestines'.

The Workshop Bugle recently carried a news report about a chap who'd happily
'recovered from a tuna of the kidney'.

An excerpt from Pulse :-
'If we are over-diagnosing asthma, then we must be under-diagnosing the other causes of nocturnal cough, such as post-natal drip'.

From a national newspaper :-
'Cutting down on fats reduces the risk of heart disease. Try to choose unsaturated fats, which are found in red meat, milk, cheese, coconut oil, palm oil and butter .

From the Daily Mail :-
'A transplant surgeon has called for a ban on "kidneys-for-ale" operations'.

From a Local Paper :-
'On the Sunday before Christmas, there will be a pot-luck supper in the church hall, followed by prayers and medication'.

From the South Wales Evening Post :-
'Cash plea to aid dyslexic children'.

An interesting health tip from Q magazine :-
'In America you can buy melatonln as a vitamin supplement. It is a hormone that your penile gland secretes when it gets dark'.

19 Years in Training
By Joan Oliver Emmer

It's never a good sign when your doctor exclaims "Oh crap" while peering intently at your mammogram on the light box. Since I was standing there in a puke-green gown open to the front – not my best look – I wasn't exactly rapid-fire response ready. I *did* manage a "Great bedside manner there, doc!" before sinking into a puke-green puddle on the examining table and listening to him explain *what* it probably was and why, despite my protestations, it was unlikely we were looking at my 20 year old son's re-absorbed twin on my mammo. Which was, in fact, somewhat of a relief, since I don't have enough money to send a second child to college at this very moment.

What it *is* is a new breast cancer – a very, very, very small breast cancer, I might add. It's slightly less than half the size of the breast cancer I had 19 years ago – a breast cancer lifetime ago, so to speak. And that original breast cancer was pretty small too. The fact that it's "new," and not a recurrence of the original cancer, is also good news (though if you want to know why, you'll just have to consult Breast Cancer for Dummies, like my own doctor does in the operating room. She props it up next to the Swiss army knife and dental floss she uses to do her magic). No matter the controversy surrounding the effectiveness of mammograms, here's a case where a mammogram did *exactly* what it was supposed to do.

Did I mention that "it's" very small?

I'll need surgery, for sure (yes, *that* kind of surgery) and that *is* kind of scary in a "No eating or drinking after midnight the night before surgery" kind of way (I'm not kidding about this – the idea of skipping my morning coffee is *terrifying* to me). But I'm generally feeling pretty positive about the whole thing. At my surgical consult, the doctor bandied about the word "Baywatch" a few times and when you're 53, who can argue with *that*?

After all, I've had 19 years to "train" for this – 19 years of watching other women handle this diagnosis in ways that were polar opposites from how *I* handled my original diagnosis (i.e., lying prostrate on the floor and babbling "Nanu Nanu" like Robin Williams in Mork and Mindy). 19 years of observing how other people deal with scary news, choosing grace and optimism rather than Valium and my typical "let's see how miserable I can make my family with my doomsday predictions" modus operandi. 19 years to understand deep within my kishkes how very fortunate I am with the particulars of this diagnosis given all the things that can go wrong in life health-wise. (That said, don't FOR ONE MINUTE think I'm too "zen" or Hari Krishna to benefit from a surprise "pity package" of chocolate).

Plus I might actually get a tummy tuck out of this particular surgery.

So since everyone is always asking "How can I help?" when someone is experiencing a challenge, and I'm a firm believer in giving people very specific tasks so that I don't end up with 15 tuna-noodle casseroles, 9 coupons for an oil change and 12 pink ribbon teddy bears (not that there's anything wrong with that), here's a list of helpful stuff my family and I could really use in the coming weeks:

$70,000 for Thing 1's final two years of college tuition. After all, a mind is a terrible thing to waste.

A new non-mini van "vehicle." I like Japanese makes and models. That tummy tuck will look much better in a shiny new sedan (with seat warmers) than in a mom-mobile.

Tickets for next year's Springsteen concert in Europe. Either London or Paris is fine – you choose.

I still reserve the right to an occasional nervous breakdown. If you help me through mine, I'll help you through yours (and I KNOW you're having them, despite looking all cool, collected and Kennedy-like). Thanks for listening. I'll be in touch – and hope you will too.

A Short History of Medicine

I have an earache...

2000 B.C. - Here, eat this root.

1000 A.D. - That root is heathen. Here, say this prayer.

1850 A.D. - That prayer is superstition. Here, drink this potion.

1940 A.D. - That potion is snake oil. Here, swallow this pill.

1985 A.D. - That pill is ineffective. Here, take this antibiotic.

2012 A.D. - That antibiotic is artificial. Here, eat this root.

My Hysterical- Ectomy
Debra Joy Hart RN BFA CLL

What do you get when you combine a nurse, a clown and uterine fibroids the size of overgrown tropical fruit?

How about just calling it all dangerous? A "hospital clown" in a hospital setting? An infection control nurse that has poked, prodded, picked and pricked every orifice known to humankind? Dangerous, dastardly and Deb would be the correct answer.

My decision to submit to this operation was easy. I was 41 years old, had L-I-S-I (laughter induced stress incontinence) and didn't need any more baby making parts.

The doc didn't have any idea what she was agreeing to.

To prepare myself as well as co workers for 6 weeks off of work, I had a body part "coming out" party. The menu included: Uterine shaped garlic cheese ball, crackers, green onion fallopian tubes, olive ovaries, jelly beans (to represent eggs) and the "piece de resistance", a Deb (me) shaped cake, outfitted with Fruit Loop ™ earrings, spikey licorice hair and a speculum (clean, in case you were wondering) as a serving tool.

I wanted to write on the sign "Eat Me", but settled for, "'Bon Appétit"

The day of the operation, or as I called it "plunk my junk", I had a surgical pen that I had scribbled next to a previous vertical abdomen scar, "CUT HERE." I found out the surgeon wanted to write back, "OOPS," but that specifically is not covered by malpractice insurance.

My hospital overnight bag included red rubber noses, oversized scissors and a 2 foot plastic thermometer. Unfortunately, 24 hours later, I was not feeling like a laugh. Pain however can be a great motivator to self medicate with humor.

I was in excruciating pain from impossible impassable flatulence and a minister came to visit me. I was rollin' from side to side and bug eyed from pain. He asks' what can I do? I said" Pray for gas, Father. Please let me fart." He didn't bat an eye at my request, he merely left the room. I'm sure he heard this prayer before. C'mon, he's a guy....all men pray to stink out their wives or girlfriends.

Nurses are really impatient patients and my pain increased, as well as my girth. I was blowing up like the Violet Beauregard in the Willie Wonka movie. The nurse was not answering my call light fast enough or with any regularity (excuse the pun). Desperate times call for desperate measures. I took a page out of my "little old lady in a nursing home" playbook. Ladies in long term care know what to do. If the nurse doesn't answer the call light within 15 seconds so that LOL (little'ol lady) can have her enema... call 911.

I scaled that back just a little, because I was pretty sure my HMO would not cover that call. However, I did dial the hospital switchboard and told her to call the 4th floor nurse and send her to room 433. I thought I was clever... and yet, my prayers were still not answered. To quote a version of Shakespeare, I could not let flee o'fart.

The morning nurse knew exactly what to do to give me some relief. The medical term for this procedure is not important or pronounceable. It did involve a large bored plastic tube and a bag of water hung from the heavens above... I think Colonel Potter did this to his horse in an episode of M.A.S. H. The outcome: I was blowing more bubbles from my butt than 12 kids in one bathtub. And, I sang the entire Hawaiian Don Ho song," Tiny Bubbles'. The heavenly angels sighed a collective "Ahhhhhhhhhhhhh" in the key of G.

Ten days later I looked at my incision, and knew my "running stitch" was ready to come out. I called the nurse and said." I have taken out hundreds of these. I just cut the end and pull, right?" What the hell was I thinking? Was I insane or just wanting to look like the hero in some spaghetti western that takes out his own stitches? I stood before the bathroom mirror, looked down at my belly, got wobbly knees and sick to my stomach. My nurse ego than took over. "Take a deep breath, hold it and don't let go until the stitches are out." It helps to talk in third person when being tough!

I pulled the 15 inch blue cord through my belly, out my nose (just kidding...about my nose) and let out my breath. I called my husband, told what I did and told him my guts were piled on the floor.

And what is any surgical procedure without a 6 week check –you- out- make- sure- you are- not- dead visit? I came prepared for more mayhem and mischief. A med student came in to examine me. I have a penchant for med students only because they are fun to psychologically torture. I poker face ask," Did they tell you about my condition?" He quickly went back to the chart, his face reading," Is she really crazy or does she have an incurable disease?" I hugged the sheet closer to my chin, faking fear, but instilling it in him. He looks at my vertical incision site and his eyes get wide. I had written (upside down, I might add) in green marker, "Thank You. Great Job!" He doesn't know if it's appropriate to laugh, so he goes and gets my regular doc. She comes in laughing... and laughs again at what is written.

All in all, the last laugh was on me. I did not read what kind of marker I had used. For the next 6 weeks," Thank You, Great Job!" greeted me every morning. What a way to heal!

After having their 11th child, an Alabama couple decided that that was enough (they could not afford a double-wide). So, the husband went to his doctor (who also treated mules) and told him that he and his wife/cousin didn't want to have any more children. The doctor told him that there was a procedure called a vasectomy that could fix the problem. The doctor instructed him to go home, get a cherry bomb light it, put it in a beer can, then hold the can up to his ear and count to 10.

The man went home, lit a cherry bomb and put it in a beer can. He held the can up to his ear and began to count. "1, 2, 3, 4, 5 . . . . ", at which point he paused, placed the beer can between his legs and resumed counting on his other hand. . .

Sometimes It *Is* Brain Surgery
David Woodside

Brain surgery is not very amusing. It does have its moments, though, like when the CAT scan image of your brain looks like Daffy Duck's face. Then you realize someone will be cutting through your skull. By "cut" I mean "rotary bone saw", and by "skull" I mean "THE HELL YOU SAY!"

I was the caregiver in charge of Daffy's brain surgery to remove a tumor on her brain near her ear. A brain surgery caregiver does many things like researching brain tumors, helping to select surgeons, studying YouTube brain surgery videos in case the surgical team is shorthanded and you're asked to help, and sending text messages to friends and family during the operation ("Hour 4: nurse says the team is a bit peckish, but otherwise doing fine. Will resume after dinner.").

In brain surgery there are almost always complications; for example, sometimes your cell phone doesn't get coverage in the waiting room. Daffy developed a spinal fluid leak. We didn't notice it for six weeks, figuring it was just normal urine leakage that happens when you get older. But no, the docs said it was brain fluid and scolded us for not noticing it was coming out of her head instead of her…well…kidney area. Another surgery was immediately performed because the doc had his tools in his pocket. This time they chased the leak path, which meandered around her inner ear, created a waterfall at the end of the eustachian tube, and finally ended in a warm pool near the hippocampus, where many small medical students were studying for anatomy finals in the courtyard.

Recovery from the second surgery took a few more days in the hospital. Finally, Daffy was proclaimed cured and was readied for discharge when I---super caregiver---said, "Maybe we should make sure there's still no brain fluid leak?" That seemed reasonable to everyone, particular the janitors who have to mop the stuff up, so a new difficult and expensive procedure was devised in which Daffy had to bend over, and then everyone watched brain fluid drip out her nose into a bucket.

Doctors flooded into the room and planned a third surgery. One said, "This time we should cut a bigger hole in front of her ear and dam the brain fluid at the source near the temporal lobe, hee hee." A second surgeon disagreed, "No, let's go back through the first hole and use beeswax. That stuff's really sticky." The third surgeon said, "No look! She's was sleeping in my bed and she's still there!" Which was quickly followed by, "Let's just sew her eustachian tube shut so the fluid can't get out her nose!" Relieved that we had not thought of such a stupid idea, we quickly agreed to the procedure.

During the recovery from the first two surgeries, every few hours of every day nurses come in to do various tests and measurements (not including checking for brain fluid leaks, which is left to the janitor). On each visit, many questions are asked: What's your name? What's your birthday? Where are you? What year is it? Eventually, every time Daffy saw a nurse, she preemptively yelled, "DAFFY ·5·9·53·UNIVERSITY HOSPITAL·TWO THOUSAND ELEVEN ·CAN I GET ANOTHER PAIN PILL FOR HELLS SAKE!"

Daffy's hearing had been damaged during the first surgery. When she was waiting outside the operating room to be wheeled in for her last surgery, a nurse came by to make sure he knew which side of Daffy's head was to be operated on. He asked, "What ear is it?" Mishearing, Daffy blasted away at the poor guy, "TWO THOUSAND ELEVEN!!!!" We had a good laugh as I pointed out all the stitches and shaved hair on the left side as being a pretty good indication of where to operate.

Recovery from the third surgery was the worst of all. It wasn't fun for Daffy either. She was hooked to many tubes and for 10 days they had to keep her brain fluid a quart low to promote healing. This is dangerous because of the risk of infection and tripping hazards. Finally on discharge day they did one last test. Daffy had to hold her breath, pressurize her brain and do her best to get fluid to leak from somewhere. Imagine our happiness to discover no brain fluid leaks! As we were leaving, though, we heard the janitor loudly wondering how so much pee got all over the walls.

A man speaks frantically into the phone, "My wife is pregnant, and her contractions are only two minutes apart!"
"Is this her first child?" the doctor queries.
"No, you idiot!" the man shouts. "This is her husband!"

Confessions of a Candy Striper
E. Mitchell

When I was sweet sixteen I was a volunteer candy striper for a local hospital. Sweet sixteen means pretty green, but before I start sounding like a Dr. Seuss poem, let me just say there was nothing poetic about my performance as a junior Florence Nightingale.

I confess to being a contender for the title "World's Worst Volunteer," shattering the myth that a warm body is better than none at all. My contribution to humanity was not only negligible, it bordered on detrimental.

Just watch the movie "Tammy and the Doctor" and you'll get some idea of the level of bumbling incompetence unleashed on the world when I showed up for work. In that movie, Tammy was depicted as an illiterate, shanty-boat bumpkin. My credentials were even worse – I was a clueless teenager.

My experience at the hospital was more like a blooper reel than a resume builder. I did everything wrong:

- -I walked in on people in various states of undress (curiously, men didn't seem to mind but the women sure did!)
- -I tried to deliver flowers to someone receiving last rites.
- -I asked new mothers in the maternity ward when they were expecting their babies. (How was I supposed to know that post-partum weight loss takes time?)
- -I told a fellow volunteer to inform visitors that the patient they were looking for had checked out because it said "expired" on the info card. The

patient had checked out all right – not only out of the hospital, but out of this world!

- -I delivered a patient to the wrong wing of the hospital.
- -I took a patient to the wrong floor and couldn't figure out why the doors were locked (it was the psychiatric ward).
- -I struggled, painfully slowly, to push a man twice my size in a wheelchair (he kept asking why it was taking so long) and when we finally reached the elevator, I discovered the brakes were on.

At least I didn't injure anyone, other than myself. Let's face it, all I had going for me was the cute, pink-and-white pinafore. And I often got that caught in the elevator doors.

Needless to say, I did not pursue a career in the Health Care field. Needless to say, the Health Care field is extremely grateful.

The patient shook his doctor's hand in gratitude and said, "Since we are the best of friends, I would not want to insult you by offering payment. But I would like for you to know that I had mentioned you in my will."

"That is very kind of you," said the doctor emotionally, and then added, "Can I see that prescription I just gave you? I'd like to make a little change."

CHART TALK #3

- Irregular heart failure
- Need to maintain dialogue with the family regarding the appropriateness of limiting futile care to the patient
- Patient was apprehended and guarded
- Pulses are fixed and dilated
- Patient responded to life maintenance questions – "Do you want your wife to receive artificial insemination?"
- Findings compatible with ileus. Bladder is still in colon
- Reason for leaving Hospital – "Patient wants to live"
- Denies any rectal breeding
- Fireballs in the uterus
- If she wants children, think about recommending birth control pills
- "Nephrolithiasis; discharge instructions, drink plenty of urine."
- Plan – gently dehydrate
- Chief complaint – bazaar behavior
- I follow him for his paranoia
- We will watch her diarrhea closely
- This is a 981 year old female with a host of medical problems.
- Order: Please feed patient only when awake.
- When asked if she had a discharge, the patient said, "No, but I have Blue Cross Blue Shield."
- He is allergic to wives.

Hip Op Album
By Chris McKerracher

My father is a great man with many wonderful qualities. I realized long ago that being the recipient of a complete set of his genes, has given me a huge vista of opportunities for receiving some pretty terrific features, both physical and psychical ... psychiatrical ... and er... non-physical. Sorry, the pain killers are kicking in again.

Anyway, some of the qualities I hoped to be bestowed on me (Live better genetically!) included wisdom and determination, intelligence and a quick wit. That "Green Thumb" Dad has been cursed with is not on the list, mind you. I can't imagine my life suddenly improving because I acquired his inexplicable insatiable drive to do gardening.

Sadly, of all possible aspects of my father to be potentially blessed with, the one I did end up receiving was an arthritic hip. On the one hand, I am deliriously happy that it wasn't that aforementioned rotor-tilling fixation. On the other, however, I am rather embarrassed that, at least Dad had an excuse for having a bum hip. Apparently jumping out of airplanes over war-torn Europe can be harder on the hips than ten pounds of Almondillos.

Meanwhile all I have to show for my bad joint are dozens of losing seasons of slow-pitch baseball. I realize one is supposed to sacrifice their body for their sport, but if you ever saw this body, I doubt you could think of a sport worthy of a sacrifice that large.

Either way, there I was last week, laying on a gurney in the hospital at 6:00 in the morning waiting for a new hip. I had already been stripped of my clothes, my valuables and my dignity, none of which they said I'd need for the next few days. I recall they did provide me with a lovely frock to wear instead; a piece of cloth with just enough snaps and straps to make you believe you could actually make such things as neck and arm holes out of. Just as I suspected, a quick look at the tag read "Manufactured by the Origami Clothing Company; a subsidiary of Ikea"

I felt uneasy about my garment as I had been assigned a shapely young lady named Pam who was a student nurse at the hospital. I'm sure her heart was warm because her hands were so cold, you would have to measure their temperature on the Kelvin scale, much like liquid nitrogen or Dick Cheney's heart. She claimed to be "thirty-ish" but I was sure she was skipping class from Junior High to be there. I would have been mortified if my microscopic, mal-adjusted hospital gown had let me down in the modesty department.

I needn't have worried. It didn't take long to learn that there's no such thing as "privacy", "decency" or people concerned about the odd wedding tackle sightings. In fact, accidental exposure is so common; you'd think you were on MTV. Thanks to those stupid gowns they make everyone wear; I haven't seen so many bums since "Free Cardboard Box Day" at the food bank.

As Pam and I chatted, a lady in a nurse's outfit came up with a little paper cup with some mystery meds in them and a small glass of some liquid that tasted like the chemical they coat sour gummies with only without the sweetness or flavour. I took the meds, of course, as requested. The "nurse" may even have told me their contents. It didn't much matter as I was already obedience mode or, as I like to call it; "Cupcake Defensive Posture". This is where I break out of my usual groove and keep my mouth shut and do exactly as I'm told. Question nothing and you might get out of here alive, I thought.

Upon taking the meds I turned to Pam. Maybe. Or maybe not because my memory doesn't go back any farther.

They must have given me their high-end anti-memory drugs because when I regained consciousness, I was already in my room in the four-man ward. I asked Pam what happened to the recovery room component of my experience and she looked at me rather oddly.

"You were in recovery for over an hour," she looked slightly miffed. "In fact, I thought we had a wonderful conversation."

She assured me, however, I hadn't said anything untoward and that I was "rather amusing" although she would not elaborate on how amusing or why.

I was amazed, if not a little concerned, over the gap in my memory. Whenever I've had a general anesthetic in the past, I could still recall everything up to the point where the guy in the mask says to count backwards from 100. I've always remembered meeting the doctors and his associates. This time, however, they blanked out an extra hour and a half or so of memory. What was most disconcerting, however, was that, afterward, a number of health care practitioners would look at me with some kind of weird recognition thing.

"Oh, Mr. McKerracher," one said, "You're that guy who…oh…tum te tum tum."

Or

"Ooooohhh… you're that guy that …er …uh…Say! It looks like it might be cloudy or not today, eh?"

I decided I was better off without pursuing it. I was a fairly happy camper; the operation appeared to be a success although I didn't ask to see the worn parts like you're supposed to do at the mechanics. I had a cute-as-a-bug's-ear nursing student at my beck and call, something none of the other guys in the ward had, although she wouldn't say why I merited my own personal attendant. Throw in as much pharmacologically induced euphoria as my brain could stomach and I was sitting pretty.

In fact, other than the oppressively painful ten-inch wound in my right thigh being held together with staples and gauze, I'd recommend the experience highly!

I will say this, however; as nice as it was when I got home, family members are not nearly as quick or gracious about getting me ice water as Pam was. Cupcake says if she is compared to Pam once more, my hip will be the least painful part of my body.

Apparently life is getting back to normal.

The tired doctor was awakened by a phone call in the middle of the night.

"Please, you have to come right over," pleaded the distraught young mother. "My child has swallowed a contraceptive."

The physician dressed quickly; but before he could get out the door, the phone rang again.

"You don't have to come over after all," the woman said with a sigh of relief. "My husband just found another one."

Wow! Nice Uvea!
(We all do it. We all hate it. No, not flossing.)

Barry Parham

I couldn't believe it. Had a whole year really passed? Really? But there it was – the appointment card from my eye doctor's, which brooked no argument. It was time for my annual eyeball tune-up and lube.

End of discussion. Facts are facts, unless you're a pathological liar, or in politics. (Yeah, I know.)

You know the drill. And you know you have to do it. Even if *you* think your eyes are fine, you know you have to go. Even if you never mistake your mom for your dad. Even if once, last month, you went a whole day without running into things. You have to honor the eye doctor's appointment card.

And you get no points at all for being able to actually *read* the appointment card.

You know the drill. Every year, you have to put aside a couple of hours to get your eyes checked out by a professional Eye Checker-Outer. They don't actually *say* "Eye Checker-Outer," of course. But for some unexplained reason, this branch of the medical profession couldn't settle for normal medical profession titles, like Dentist, or Pediatrician, or Demon Barber. So they putzed around with a Latin version of Boggle until they had enough syllables to call themselves Ophthalmologists (literal translation: Opthal Checker-Outer).

Step one, of course, once you arrive at the Opthalicron, is to peer through the little sliding-glass window at an empty check-in desk. Eventually, someone will drift past the desk, possibly by mistake, and immediately not notice you (maybe they should go get *their* eyes checked). After some undefined period of time, the lady (it's always a lady), who's wearing some kind of loose-fitting outfit stamped with Flintstones cartoon characters (it's always either the Flintstones or Scooby-Doo), will not look directly at you and ask you if your insurance has changed.

Your insurance status is what defines what will happen, or won't happen, next. Your insurance status is more important than incidental trivia like your name, how your kids are doing in school, or the fact that you're bleeding freely from the forehead and holding your detached left leg in your right arm.

It doesn't help matters, either, that Flintstone Lady always seems just a tiny bit bitter (perhaps due to having made a career choice that involves going to lunch five days a week with other ladies, all wearing loose-fitting Flintstone pajamas).

Anyway, after you've scribbled through the formalities, Flintstone Lady ushers you into the examining chamber, a dimly-lit windowless room inevitably decorated, like all medical and dental facilities, in a neutral-colors theme so foul that you can actually buy it at Home Depot, should you have such an aberrant urge (just ask for Early Appalachian Orthodontia). This color scheme is the result of years of secret CIA research in psychological warfare, designed to turn the targeted human into a pliant dweeb who will numbly accept commands like "Yes, everything but your underwear" and "Okay, now spit."

There's something about that chair in the eye doctor's examining room that makes the visitor feel like an undersized space alien, about to be questioned or … gulp … probed. You're sitting there in the semi-darkness, surrounded by lots of looming, off-white machinery, as if you'd been kidnapped and spirited off to some sort of evil Swivel Museum.

After tapping a computer keyboard for a while, Flintstone Lady felt her way over to my ecto-chair and, with no explanation whatsoever, handed me a preparatory Kleenex. She began to manipulate the machine's eerily organic elements, all of which required me to "rest your chin here," a phrase I haven't heard since watching a very dismal Lifetime Channel mini-series about the French Revolution.

For a while, we played some kind of weird game where she Gatling-gunned slides at me and kept yelling, "Better? Or worse?"

I never did find out my score.

Finally, Flintstone Lady zapped me with a three-gallon dose of eye drops, turned on a little projector, and made me read very tiny, incredibly misspelled words.

This is it? This is the pinnacle of progress in medical science? You're sitting in a dark closet with a mildly bitter adult. Your eyes are dripping some kind of eye-drop residue the consistency of queso and the color of three-week-old sun-dried ferret. And you're being forced to recite words like "LZ3VRTSX" to a professional wearing pajamas.

By the time Flintstone Lady's silhouette made her exit, my eyes looked like an Audrey Hepburn movie poster. I was so dilated I was afraid I might go into labor.

In spite of it all, though, going to the eye doctor's office beats going to the "full-body-contact" doctor's office in three important ways. Firstly, you don't have to get weighed. Secondly, you don't have to take off all your clothes, put on a gown that would show off your cleavage if your cleavage was on your back, and sit, shivering, on a roll of generic gift-wrapping paper.

The other advantage of visiting the eye doctor's is a conspicuous absence of specimen cups. If you're ever at an eye doctor's office, and any Scooby-Doo'd staffer hands you a specimen cup, you should demand to see some ID. Or just tell them you have no insurance.

Finally, the doctor himself, the actual Optimal Thologist, decided to drop by. He asked how my insurance was doing; had I experienced any blurred vision; had I noticed any running into poles and nearby people.

I did get some good news, though. I think. I'm not sure, because by this point the eye drops were puddling in my ears, but I think the eye doc said I might get an early Cadillac.

Then he handed me a bill for the Kleenex, opened the closet door, and disappeared into a halo of light.

Minutes passed. Machinery hummed. A speaker in the ceiling looped through bad orchestral arrangements of Neil Diamond tunes, but I was too dilated to escape. In my mind, I began to organize my last will and testament. I calmed my soul.

Not to worry. Flintstone Lady finally re-materialized and outfitted me with an embarrassingly cheesy dark-glasses device – a temporary, die-cut piece of light-defying plastic that was supposed to cling to my glasses and protect my poor, dilated eyeballs from sunlight, as long as I avoided sunlight.

The faux glasses did *not* deliver – I merely transitioned from living in a blurred world to living in a blurred, dark world. All the glasses accomplished was to shield my face while cursing at daylight, while simultaneously making me look like Will Smith playing Ray Charles, but less rich.

I couldn't focus, I certainly couldn't drive, and I was behaving like Will Smith playing Helen Keller, but less cute. So, for the rest of morning, I sat on a bench outside the office, holding a specimen cup and singing the blues.

Not a bad morning, as it turned out. I pulled down twenty-eight bucks.

That'll almost cover the Kleenex.

World's Worst Doctor Jokes

Doctor, I think I need glasses.
You certainly do, this is Mexican restaurant.

Doctor, I think I'm a bell.
Take these and if it doesn't clear up give me a ring.

Doctor, will this ointment really clear up my acne?
I never make rash promises.

Doctor, I'm suffering from Déjà vu.
Didn't I see you yesterday?

Doctor, my son swallowed my pen. What should I do?
Use a pencil until I get there.

Saving Soles
Dorothy Rosby

When a medical professional says, "You need surgery," many thoughts race through your mind, the main one being, "Isn't there an easier way to get some time off?"

In my case, the nurse even showed me a matter-of-fact video about the procedure the doctor was recommending. I think this was meant to make my upcoming double bunionectomy seem as easy as having my tires rotated. Still I left the doctor's office in a daze, tormented by all the questions I WISHED I'd asked. And to make matters worse, someone called the day before the surgery to ask me a long list of questions, including whether I have advanced directives and a living will. I said, "Wait a minute! I'm having foot surgery."

"This is just to be on the safe side."

"Whose safe side?"

This conversation did nothing to help me sleep that night. And I thought, "I SHOULD sleep." Then I thought "Why? I'm not the one doing the work tomorrow."

I reported to the surgery center the next morning very tired and with nothing but the clothes on my back--and not even my best ones. As you know, women are instructed not to wear jewelry or make-up on surgery day. And to be fair, I don't think men should either.

Women will also have been told not to bring a purse. And as any woman will tell you, being without your purse is like being naked. In short order you're that way too. Of course, I was given a gown (warmer than the paper ones you wear in a clinic, but not as attractive).

I was led into a large room filled with busy medical professionals dressed in colorful clothing. And I remember thinking, "How nice that they all wear colors now instead of white like they did long ago. It's so much more cheerful. And color won't show the blood as badly." And then I remember thinking, "I wish I didn't think so much."

A nice man, wearing what looked like pajamas, told me he was going to give me something to help me relax. Then I quit thinking altogether.

Eventually, I woke up feeling like I wanted to sleep—very similar to the way I feel on Monday mornings. Nurses came and went. I didn't care. They did things to me. I didn't care. When the anesthesia wore off, they sent me home with a lovely pair of surgical shoes. One size doesn't quite fit all—but one shoe does fit either foot.

Then came recovery. The flowers and painkillers, the attention and time off were all very nice, but I think it would have been less expensive and more interesting to take a cruise. I wasn't even fully recovered when the bills started arriving. There were bills from the surgery clinic, the doctor, the anesthesiologist, the lab, and the manufacturer of the surgical shoes. For once, something exceeded credit card offers in my mailbox. This did nothing to aid in my recovery. Not only could I not pay all the bills, I couldn't understand them. That's probably why so many people who, after having a life-saving procedure, just go ahead and die.

Recovery wasn't all bad though. I spent a month with my feet up, reading, playing solitaire, and ordering my husband around—which normally I would NEVER do.

I soon learned that daytime television is perfect for sick people and people under the influence of painkillers—because apparently it's created by sick people—sick, sick people and people under the influence ... of something.

I learned that playing army with my son, a game I've not always enjoyed, is more enjoyable when I get to lie on the couch and pretend to be a wounded soldier.

And I learned how gratifying it is to say, "Honey, WHILE YOU'RE UP, could you ..." I LOVE that. My husband has often used that on me and now I know why. WHILE YOU'RE UP, could you get me a cup of tea? WHILE YOU'RE UP, could you turn up the heat? WHILE YOU'RE UP, could you paint the house?

This was so pleasant that I started to envision a very long recovery. I pictured myself welcoming visitors from my place on the couch, and saying pitifully, "Please forgive me if I don't get up; I just had surgery."

They would say, "I'm sorry! When?" and I would answer, "Nine years ago. Could you hand me that cheese dip—WHILE YOU'RE UP?"

The seven-year old girl told her mom, "A boy in my class asked me to play doctor."
"Oh, dear," the mother nervously sighed. "What happened, honey?"
"Nothing, he made me wait 45 minutes and then double-billed the insurance company."

A Night on the Run

Jan Hurst-Nicholson

There is never a good time to get the trots. And a long weekend in a full caravan park is definitely not one of them.

I'm no gastronaut. I like my food plain, and avoid anything on the menu that has to be explained. So I put it down to the take-away salad. The olives to be precise. My wife, who had generously given me her share, had not become similarly afflicted.

It was 21:30 when I became uncomfortably aware that my digestive system was not all it should be. I crawled miserably into the sleeping bag.

By 22:30 cramping pains warned that serious internal mischief was afoot. Like a caterpillar emerging from a cocoon I slithered out of the sleeping bag and clambered over my gently snoring partner. Torch in hand I unlocked the door and stepped into the inky blackness. A sullen yellow light glowed dimly from the ablution block. I tiptoed along the gravel path, fearful of waking slumbering neighbours.

Feeling a slight sense of relief I re-emerged into the darkness, only to suffer a near relapse when a spectre-like figure loomed out of the shadows and manifested itself before me. A low growl announced the welcome presence of the security man and his trusty canine partner. We nodded companionably and he was swallowed up in the night.

I'd hardly settled back into the sleeping bag when internal rumblings forced a repeat trip, this time requiring a little more alacrity. I tried negotiating a shorter route between neighbouring vans, but a netting of guy ropes and lethally positioned steel pegs had me blundering about like a myopic hedgehog. I barely made it in time. The dreaded Diarrhoea &Vomiting was upon me.

I hoped that no one else had partaken of the olives. This was not the time to be forming queues.

I needed liquids. But my wife, having been advised to treat all water with suspicion, had added judicious amounts of sterilising fluid to our storage tank. It was like drinking swimming pool water. I opted to risk it straight from the tap. If anything scurrilous lurked in its contents it wouldn't linger long enough to cause any further ill effects.

As midnight approached I was prancing back and forth like Michael Flatley on speed. The guard dog's growl had now turned to a wag of recognition and I considered including him in my holiday snapshots.

For the sake of convenience, I gave up closing the caravan door. If someone came in to murder me they would be welcome. The torch was coming out in sympathy, its beam as weak as I felt. I lay motionless in the sleeping bag, afraid even to cough.

I am not one to suffer in silence. I find it comforting to give the occasional groan, interspersed with whimpers of self-pity. My wife, usually the epitome of solicitous sympathy during the day, does not take kindly to having her sleep disturbed.

"Must you make those noises. There's no point in both of us being awake all night."

I groaned into a pillow before setting off on yet another excursion. It had to be dysentery at the very least.

A further encounter with the security guard had me mentally adding him to my Christmas card list.

By the feeble light of the torch I searched through my wife's medical Pandora of insect repellents, plasters, cough lozenges, massage oil for stiff muscles, headache remedies and sun block. There was nothing remotely suggesting a cure for D & V. Caravan parks are not known for their proximity to emergency chemists, and it would be pushing neighbourliness to knock on caravan doors at 04h00 expecting a lift into the nearest town. I curled up on the floor and awaited death.

As the sun gradually nudged in a new day I was mentally ticking off the people who could be expected to attend my funeral.

It wasn't long before the smell of fried bacon and sausages was drifting nauseatingly on the morning air.

My wife, refreshed after a night's sleep, was all loving concern. She brewed up an Oral Rehydration Salts solution of sugar, salt and water, and even cut the crusts off the slice of dry bread that was all I could face.

It wasn't long before fellow campers heard of my predicament. Ever helpful, they rallied round and came up with a selection of remedies. Weak, but continent, I lived through the day.

My wife, suffering sympathy fatigue, vowed there would be no more take-away salads. Bottled water was top of the shopping list.

I spent the rest of the weekend thumbing through the 'Guide to Caravan Parks', determined the next resort we visited would have private ablution facilities.

Stop Smacking the Little Guy
Mike Cyra

I laid my pen down and turned in my seat. There stood one of the Mexican processors with his pants around his ankles and his penis in his hand.

I instantly pushed my chair two feet backwards. "What's the problem?" I asked. He had a worried look on his face and said, "The head of my deek, it is all red."

I thought of saying, "use some Vaseline next time," but instead I looked down at it and nodded. "Certainly is."

He just stared at me and said in broken English, "And I can no feel eet." He looked down at his little red friend and then back up at me, "Why es my deek red?"

I looked up at the ceiling and thought to myself, "why me?" Why? Because for eight years I was the Chief Medical Officer on the largest fish processing mother ship in the United States. A six hundred eighty foot, 17,000-ton ship with over 200 crewmembers who worked 24 hours a day, seven days a week. And this worried individual was one of my patients.

"How long has it been red?" I asked. He replaced the stranglehold he had on his penis with the other hand and scratched his chin. "Oh, maybe two years."

What in the hell is he talking about? I suppressed a smile and asked, "So your penis has been red for two years and numb for two days?" He gave me a look that said, "What the hell are you talking about"

I couldn't remember the Spanish word for numb so I tried, "When you say you can't feel it, you mean like it is asleep?" This he understood, "Sí!" With his free hand he reached down and smacked the head of his penis four or five times. Harder than I had ever seen anyone hit their penis intentionally. "Sí, asleep, I can no feel."

I really wanted to say, "Well you keep slapping the damn thing like that no wonder you can't feel it and no wonder it's red." But I chose a more clinical question, "Have you been doing anything with it, you know, playing with it?"

"No no." He answered like I had just asked him if he had waxed his car today. Which, in a way, I guess is what I was asking him.

"Have you been having sex on the boat?" He got a very serious look on his face and said, "Oh nooooo!" I asked, "Have you had this problem before? Has your penis gone to sleep before?"

Holding the base of it with his right hand, he stretched it out and smacked it with his left hand and said, "No, no, just for two days now."

I couldn't take it anymore, "Don't do that! Do you always smack it like that?" He looked at me with a blank expression, "No, no". I looked up to God, "What did I do God, Huh? What did I do?"

By this time I didn't know what the hell to ask him. I've done my rotations through the "Crotch Watch" departments, and I've been to all the "Pecker Checker" classes, but they didn't cover this.

"Is the whole thing asleep?" He looked at it and said, "Sí, they head and they long part, ah...they shaft. It es hot too, feel it." He offered it to me like it was a cigarette.

I rolled my chair back another foot and said, "No I don't need to do that just yet. I can see it and it certainly looks hot and numb and red from here."

I thought maybe he wanted me to smack the shit out of it too, maybe smack it with a book just to make sure it was numb.

I wished I were in a hospital full of doctors so I could send this guy to one I didn't like. But, I was in the middle of the Bering Sea.

I went through a litany of questions trying to get some type of handle on what might be going on. He kept a tight grip on it and occasionally looked down and flicked it with his finger, like how you flick a bug off your arm. Over and over he flicked the head of his poor, numb, red penis.

I told him, "You can pull up your pants now." Before he did, he gave the head one last whack and said, "I can no feel."

I told him, "You gotta stop smacking your deek like that man!" He just looked at me with that blank expression, so I told him the thing you always say to patients when you don't have the foggiest idea what's going, on or what to say.

"Why don't we just watch it for a couple of days and see what happens and you let me know how you're doing ok?" He seemed ok with that and said, "Sí, OK, thank you."

I told him he shouldn't worry too much and that I would see him in a couple of days, although I really hoped I wouldn't.

That afternoon I called the Physician I consult with on the ship to shore satellite phone. I told him about this patient and he asked me, "Did you tell him to use Vaseline next time?"

We decided that neither one of us knew of any medical condition that would cause this except smacking the head of your dick every few minutes, which isn't a medical condition. That's just abusing your penis.

I passed this patient in the hall a couple of days later and I asked him, "How are you doing, how is...you know?"

He broke out in a big smile and said, "Oh everything es just fine, they stuff you gave me worked bueno, thank you," and he walked away.

I didn't recall giving him anything but I was just happy he didn't want me to watch him smack his deek anymore.

Loeb's first law of medicine says; "If what your doing is working, keep doing it!"

Welcome to the Psychiatric Hotline

If you are obsessive-compulsive, please press 1 repeatedly.

If you are co-dependent, please ask someone to press 2.

If you have multiple personalities, please press 3, 4, 5, and 6.

If you are paranoid-delusional, we know who you are and what you want. Just stay on the line so we can trace the call.

If you are schizophrenic, listen carefully and a little voice will tell you which number to press.

If you are manic-depressive, it doesn't matter which number you press. No one will answer.

If you are anxious, just start pressing numbers at random.

If you are phobic, don't press anything.

If you are anal retentive, please hold.

Things You Don't Want To Hear During Surgery

- Better save that. We'll need it for the autopsy.

- Someone call the janitor. We're going to need a mop.

- Hand me that, uh, that uh, thingie.

- Oh no! I just lost my Rolex.

- Oops! Hey, has anyone ever survived 500ml of this stuff before?

- Darnn, there go the lights again.

- Ya know, there's big money in kidneys. Heck, this guy's got two of 'em.

- Everybody stand back! I lost my contact lens!

- I hate it when they're missing stuff in here.

- That's cool! Now can you make his leg twitch?!

- I wish I hadn't forgotten my glasses.

- Well folks, this will be an experiment for us all.

- Sterile, shcmerile. The floor's clean, right?

- Anyone see where I left that scalpel?

- Accept this sacrifice, O Great Lord of Darkness.

- Okay, now take a picture from this angle. This is truly a freak of nature.

- Did this patient sign the organ donation card?

- She's gonna blow! Everybody take cover!!!

- Dang! Page 47 of the manual is missing!

Things You Don't Want To Hear During Your Colonoscopy

- Take it easy, Doc. You're boldly going where no man has gone before!

- Find Amelia Earhart yet?

- Can you hear me NOW?

- Are we there yet? Are we there yet? Are we there yet?

- You know, in Arkansas , we're now legally married.

- Any sign of the trapped miners, Chief?

- You put your left hand in, you take your left hand out...

- Hey! Now I know how a Muppet feels!

- If your hand doesn't fit, you must quit!

- Hey Doc, let me know if you find my dignity.

- You used to be an executive at Enron, didn't you?

- God, now I know why I am not gay.

- Could you write a note for my wife saying that my head is not up there?

Signs You Have Joined A Cheap HMO
From "Placebo"

- Dialysis machines powered by patients on treadmills.
- Use of antibiotics deemed an "unauthorized experimental procedure"
- Head wound victim in the waiting room is on the last chapter of "War and Peace"
- Annual chest x-ray conducted at Hooters.
- Exam room has a tip jar
- You swear you saw salad tongs and a crab fork on the instrument tray just before the anesthesia kicked in.
- "Will you be paying in eggs or pelts?"
- "Take two leeches and call me in the morning"
- The company logo features a hand squeezing a bleeding turnip.
- Tongue depressors taste faintly of Fudgesicle
- Covered postnatal care consists of leaving your baby on Mia Farrow's doorstep
- "Pre-natal vitamin" prescription is a box of Tic-Tacs
- Chief Surgeon graduated from University of Benihana
- Directions to your doctor's office include, "Take a left when you enter the campground"
- Doctor listens to your heart through a paper towel tube.
- Only item listed under Preventive Care feature of coverage is, "an apple a day"
- You can get your flu shot as soon as "The hypodermic needle is dry."

OUR AMAZING CONTRIBUTORS
(A.K.A. Humorists On Meds)

Barb Best feels your pain. An Erma Bombeck Global Humor Winner and a Top 10 in The Robert Benchley Humor Competition, her comedy material has been performed by Joan Rivers and published in numerous print and online magazines such as **More.com** and **Divinecaroline.com**. You'll enjoy her eBook *"100 Fast & Funny: Ha-Musings by Barb Best"* and her piece "Report Card" in the perennial hit humor anthology *"My Funny Valentine."* You can subscribe to her LOL humor blog on pop culture and entertainment at **BarbBest.com** and stalk her on Twitter *@HaBarb*.

Cindy Brown is a freelance humor writer in the Midwest, raising a husband, two kids, and two Great Pyrenees dogs. She airs her funny laundry on her blog **EverydayUnderwear.com**. Her work has also been syndicated on, **BlogHer.com**, **LunchBreakBlog.com**, and Rachel Thompson's influential site, **RachelintheOC.com**. She can be followed avidly at **@hiyacynthia**.

Richard Brown is the author of *Send In the Clown Car: The Race to the White House 2012* and *Europe On $500 a Day (And Other Reasons to Stay Home)*, which were published under his blogger name Cranky Cuss. He is retired after 23 years in the corporate world. He lives in the suburbs of New York with a wife who calls him her "first husband" and two daughters who insist they are adopted.

Dan Burt is an ardent bibliophile, but don't say so out loud because he suspects it is illegal in his home state of Alabama, where he currently lives underground with his wife and two sons. Not only is Dan imbued with fancy book learnin' junk, he's also quite experienced in the way of the world. Dan is the creator of the humor website **Captain Canard, www.CaptainCanard.com**. You can follow him on Twitter **@danburt.**

Deb Claxton What do zombies, the Mayan Calendar, deathbed confessions, and Christmas have in common? They're just some of the subjects Deb Claxton tackles in her humor collection, *"It Ain't Heavy–It's The Lite Side"* available at Amazon.com: a compilation of her newspaper column. She retired from the newspaper business but continues to spread her wacky world view through her blog, **www.debclaxton.com.** She's also on Facebook and Twitter **@calendarday**. When not writing, Claxton spends most of her time waiting in doctor's offices for the news that another body part is nearing its expiration date.

Mike Cyra is a crash-tested humor writer and author of the bestselling eBook- *Emergency Laughter: It Wasn't Funny When It Happened, But it is Now!* Mike is a former Emergency Medical Technician, Bering Sea Medic, Surgical Technologist and Instructor. His comedic stories of medicine have appeared in **the Placebo Journal, Our USA Magazine, Parenting Humor, HumorPress.com, (614)Magazine** and has received numerous awards including America's Funniest Humorpress. Mike's essay in Britain's Dying Matters 2012 international creative writing competition received a Highly Commended award and was published in the book-***Final Chapters: Writing About The End Of Life.*** He is currently finishing his next Emergency Laughter book.

Joan Oliver Emmer is a market researcher, budding social worker, blogger and Trophy Wife. She hopes one day to develop a comedy routine invoking all four identities, in the form of a monologue or, more, likely, a Greek tragedy accompanied by an off-key chorus. She is also mother to two boys, who go by the code names Thing 1 and Thing 2 to protect their identities (obviously). Read more about Joan and her life living large in New Jersey at, not surprisingly, **www.JoanOliverEmmer.com.**

Robert Ferrell is author of well over two books. He also has won awards as a calligrapher and fine artist, bookbinder, iconographer, photographer, woodworker, and semi-finalist at the 2011 Robert Benchley Society Humor Writing award. He is a classically-trained percussionist and performs with many musical ensembles, including the folk-rock group **Restless Wind**. His books, variously described as "brainy fiction," "bitingly clever social satire," and "File Not Found," are ***"Tangent"*** and ***"Infinite Loop***," the tongue-in-cheek fantasy novel ***"Goblinopolis,"*** the award-winning hallucinogenic novella ***"Infinity or Bust,"*** all on amazon.com and/or Scribd.com.

Debra Joy Hart has been in health care for over 25 years, juggling her skills as a humorist, nurse, certified laughter leader, clown and lay minister. She created the 1000 Red Nose Project, traveling the world handing out clown noses to promote peace, laughter and healthy humor. She contributed to the **21 Peaceful Nurses;**

Essays on a Spiritually Guided Practice anthology. And has been in the finals of several competitions on **humorpress.com**. Her health/humor blog is at www.debrajoyhart.com

Stacey Hatton has had 5 head concussions (that she knows of) which has led her to a conflicting career path of comedy writing, pediatric nursing and musical theatre. She is a humorist for **The Kansas City Star** newspaper and writes kids health and parenting articles, which often tend to be funnier. Ms. Hatton is a public speaker, when spoken to, and a great listener which, remarkably shows up great on paper and the web. She's a member of the Society of Children's Books and Illustrators, the National Society of Newspaper Columnists and an active "class clown" at the Erma Bombeck Writer Workshops. Check out her blog at **www.nursemommylaughs.com**. Now.

Kate Heidel is a humor writer and one-time Jersey Girl who steered clear of any Real Housewives of Jersey Shore by moving to Minneapolis. She has been writing her funny/scary humor for years, notably her regular columns in the presumably satiric **Happy Woman Magazine**, **CAP News**, the aptly named **Postcards from the Pug Bus**, and has had her work translated into French for the arty French send-up of Vogue-like mags, **Nunuche**. Ground Zero for Kate's post-edgy humor is her site, **www.wearyourcape.com**, which since 2009 has partnered with **HumorFeed**, a provider of daily humor and news satire.

Cammy May Hunnicutt is first and foremost a Southern Belle (though currently at large). She is also a total bitch. Or so her admirers say. Her debut book,

"Considerations Prior To Shooting Your Boyfriend Right In The Nuts" has been selling pretty well, considering. How funny it is seems to depend a lot on one's personal perspective (i.e. "gender"). Her serial online memoir *"Dirty Undies"* can be viewed at her site **cammymay.com**

El Kartun is a *nombre de pluma* much better known in Mexico than his given name, Jesus Pedroza. Though a fine artist and instructor on the side, El Kartun is Tijuana's most dominant cartoonist. The dean of strolling caricaturists, he also draws the only regular local comic strip for the daily "**El Sol de Tijuana**". His book, *"Just Wake Up!"* is a unique and innovative melange of graphic novel, comic, and literature.

Allen Klein is the world's only "Jollytologist," and author of 18 books that have sold over 500,000 copies. Those books include: *The Healing Power of Humor, The Courage to Laugh, Learning to Laugh When You Feel Like Crying, Inspiration for a Lifetime, Change Your Life!: A Little Book of Big Ideas,* and *The Art of Living Joyfully.* Klein is also a professional speaker and the recipient of a Lifetime Achievement Award from the **Association for Applied and Therapeutic Humor.** Comedian Jerry Lewis has said that Allen Klein **is** "a noble and vital force watching over the human condition." Klein and his work can be found at **www.allenklein.com**

Ben Link is a freelance blogger for **NatGeo TV** and **Points In Case.** You can follow him at **BinLeenk.Tumblr.com/ and BinLeenk** on Twitter. A graduate of the Upright Citizen's Brigade (L.A. improv) he was also a staff writer for iO-West's **Mainstage Sketch Show**. Ben lives in Atlanta and is always up for a good collaboration.

Pete Malicki is a fiction author, multi-award-winning playwright and notable arts administrator. He's completed five novels and over 40 plays, which have been produced in close to 100 productions around the world. He runs the world's largest festival of 10 minute plays, **Short+Sweet Sydney**, and is the organization's International Literary Manager. In 2009 he founded **Helm Publishing** and produced a novel and an illustrated children's book, then settled on editing fiction manuscripts. His playwriting awards have included Best Drama, Best Comedy, Best Play, Overall People's Choice, and Judges' Choice at various theatre festivals. Read more of his work at **www.petemalicki.com**.

Chris McKerracher is a humorist, playwright, comedian and award-winning film producer. His humor column has appeared in a number of Alberta newspapers since 1994. Chris founded the **Calmar Prairie Players theatre troupe** in 2005. Plays to his credit include ***"Calmar; Zero to Fifty in Ninety Minutes," "The 1984 Dalmar Biker War"* and *"The Dangers of VD (Valentines Day)"*** See more of Chris at his website: **http://chrismckerracher.yolasite.com/**

Dan McQuinn is an alumnus of Second City's writing program and has contributed to the writing of many plays and many unfinished crossword puzzles. Dan's first book, ***Kids Say the Cutest Things When They're***

Drunk, is a sharply written collection of comic letters, monologues and playlets that provides sure-fire laughs, drunk or sober. Dan lives in the western suburbs of Chicago with his trophy wife, two children and a dog that barks at drywall. Additional information on Dan and his writings may be found at **www.danmcquinn.com**. Dan also invites you to follow him on Twitter **@danmcquinnbytes**.

E. Mitchell is an award-winning humorist, novelist, playwright-ist with literary bling from Thurber House, the Robert Benchley Society and the Will Rogers Writers' Workshop. Anthologies include **Chicken Soup** and **A Cup of Comfort** as well as non-brothy books like "***Bad Austen***," and "In the Peanut Gallery with Mystery Science Theater 3000." E. (e. for short) is author of the sci-fi humor novel "***The Amazing, Incredible Shrinking Colossal Bikini-Crazed Creature from the Public Domain***," recently adapted for the stage in San Diego and Chicago, heading for Broadway via the Donner Pass. The 2010 Writer's Digest screenwriting awardee currently dishes the **Film Hound** blog for the **Seattle Post-Intelligencer**. Seek further befuddlement at **www.emitchellhumor.com**.

Jim Mullen writes a syndicated column that appears in over 600 newspapers across the U.S. and Canada each week. His latest book, ***How to Lose Money in Your Spare Time – At Home*** is a collection of his funniest columns over the last ten years. Jim's memoir, ***It Takes a Village Idiot,*** was a finalist for the 2001 **Thurber Prize for American Humor**. His spoof of a baby showers, ***Baby's First Tattoo*** is now in its fifteenth printing. His

Hot Sheet column ran in **Entertainment Weekly** and his work has appeared **in The New York Times, New York Magazine, The Village Voice**. He lives in Franklin, NY. His books are available in all the usual places, as well **as JimMullenBooks.com**

Jan Hurst-Nicholson wrote for South African magazines for years, much of it compiled into *Something to Read on the Plane.* Her humorous novel on adapting from Liverpool to Durban, *But Can You Drink The Water?* has been joined by award-winning *Leon Chameleon: PI* children's books, YA Mystery *Mystery At Ocean Drive*, and the family saga *The Breadwinners*, as well as many other books from Penguin and Cambridge University Press. Jan's writing also appears in **Edge Words** (stories from the Cheshire Prize for Literature), **Chicken Soup,** and **Summer Shorts.** She lives in Durban with two dogs that are forever on the wrong side of the door, an elderly cat, and the occasional visiting troop of boisterous vervet monkeys. See more about Jan and her many books at **www.just4kix.jimdo.com.**

Barry Parham writes humorous columns, essays and short stories. Music fanatic, 1981 graduate of the University of Georgia, and self-described eco-narcissist, Barry won several awards for the stories, **"Going Green, Seeing Red"** and **"Driving Miss Conception,"** in his 2009 sleeper, *"Why I Hate Straws."* To find out why he hates straws, and experience his other humorous collections, *"Sorry, We Can't Use Funny,"* and the Politically Incorrigible *"Blush: Politics and Other*

Unnatural Acts," as well as follow his columns and appearances, see Barry's author page on **amazon.com**.

Saralee Perel is a longtime lover of Cape Cod. For 15 years, her column appears regularly in the Cape Cod Times and is syndicated in 44 newspapers nationwide. To date, she has had 35 stories published in ***Chicken Soup for the Soul,*** and is a regular essayist for **The Christopher and Dana Reeve foundation.** Her columns have appeared in **Family Circle, Woman's World, Pet Gazette, Dallas News** and a host of other publications. Among other top national awards, Saralee is a four-time winner of the **National Society of Newspaper Columnists** annual contest. The **NSNC** is the largest columnist organization in the United States. She was recently honored to be selected as the **Erma Bombeck Humor Writer of the Month.** Saralee has just launched her new book: ***Cracked Nuts & Sentimental Journeys: Stories From a Life Out of Balance***. She's delighted to receive rave reviews. For info, please visit her website: **www.saraleeperel.com**.

Linton Robinson has written humor articles for newspapers, syndicates, and national magazines since the first ice age, and gotten little more than awards and suspicion to show for it. He currently resides in Mexico, which is a rich source of humor that nobody will read. His cult Nineties humor column **The Way of the Weekend Warrior**, has been converted to a widely-reviled novel and is available on amazon and **www.adorobooks.com**

Dorothy Rosby is a speaker and humorist whose column has appeared in newspapers in ten Midwestern and Western states since 1996. (The area is home to more cows than people, so the reader should not be overly impressed.) A former radio announcer, she was once asked by an employer to change her on-air name because "No one will take you seriously with a name like Dorothy." All of this has led to self-esteem issues that can only be dealt with by a healthy dose of self-deprecating humor. A two-time winner of the **South Dakota Press Women's Communications Contest/Humor Column** category and second place winner in the **2010 National Federation of Press Women Communications** contest, Dorothy also writes for **Exceptional People Magazine** and **Black Hills Woman** magazine. Learn more at her website at **www.dorothyrosby.com**.

Connie Sedona is the author of *Prescription for Laughter: Medical Humor that's Off the Charts*, a collection of "bloopers" drawn from her many years doing medical transcription. Since retiring from spotting the malaprops of medicos, she lives in the Bay Area with LucyLu and Orca, her two cats, does pet sitting part-time, and heads for the coast any chance she gets. Her book can be found on amazon.com, Kindle store, and stashed in the drawers of hospital personnel.

Jonathan Shipley is a freelance writer living in Seattle with his wonderful daughter. His play, "**Deviled Eggs,**" a humorous look at his painful romantic life, was produced and performed at the Blue Heron Theatre. His poetry has been published in a German welding magazine. Seriously. It was romantic poetry for welders. He is currently at work on a novel about cubicle life and finding words in the dictionary that'll make his daughter giggle. Jonathan's prolific work is widely published, including the **Los Angeles Times, the Boston Globe, Diner Journal, Fine Books Magazine, Lexus Magazine**, and the **Boston Globe**. Not to mention **Hobart Pulp, Seattle Salmon, Yankee Potroast** and **Cap'n Wacky**. Other anthologies include "**Mountain Man Dance Moves**," and "**The McSweeney's Joke Book of Book Jokes**." He edited the book "**Bat Boy Exposed**" for the Weekly World News. More on this amazing, weirdo, writer can be experienced at **www.jonathanshipley.blogspot.com**.

E. C. Stilson is the author of several novels including *The Golden Sky, Bible Girl & the Bad Boy* and *Crazy Life of a Writing Mom*. She spends most of her time taking care of four rambunctious kids who are better than green eggs and ham. They're pretty darnn fun, but despite that, after she had kids, her boobs shrunk, she lost hair, but gained a greater sense of humor! When she's not scavenging through the vents, where her son—The Zombie Elf—likes hiding things, she's sewing, playing her violin, editing or writing. You can see her blog at **ecwrites.blogspot.com,** her author website at **www.ecstilson.com** and her Twittering **@ ECwrites**

Karla Telega is the award-winning author of *Box of Rocks,* a humorous murder mystery. She is a graduate of the University of Washington, the class of too long ago to remember. Karla is a regular contributor to the nationally syndicated **Skirt Magazine** and has won numerous awards in the national **Humorpress** writing contest. You can read Karla's humor blog at **telegatales.com**. Look for *Box of Rocks* at amazon.com.

Lisa Tognola is a Jersey Girl, sharing her views on everything from marriage to morals to mistresses, Tognola highlights the humorous side of suburban life: the good, the bad, and the ugly. Think Erma Bombeck meets the Ladies of Wisteria Lane. Lisa's column at The Alternative Press is called "**Main Street Musings,**" but her own blog has the classier title, **Main Street Musings Blog**. Equal parts lark and snark, her musings prove the funniest things happen in the suburbs, beyond dinner at Applebee's. Her work can also be seen at online magazine **More.com**. Lisa is also a contributor to **Funny Times newspaper**. Follow her on twitter **@lisatognola**.

Dawn Weber is a Buckeye lifer who graduated from Springfield Local High School in 1987 then went on to get a bachelor's degree from Kent State University, where she majored in flammable, piece-of-shit cars and cheap beer. She currently resides in Brownsville (Motto: Indoor Plumbing Optional) with the husband, kids and an ever-changing series of dirty, ill-mannered pets. Her resume includes work at newspapers, corporations and state government, but she's resentful about that. Her goals include thinner thighs, a nap, maybe a solo trip to Walmart. Dawn's humor has been delighting readers of her "**Lighten Up!**" column in the **Buckeye Lake Beacon**, which has won awards that don't seem to impress anybody, even her. It's well worth following her **www.lightenupweber.blogspot.com**, blog unless you are a faint-at-heart wuss.

Ernie Witham is a humor lifer. A contributor to a dozen of the **Chicken Soup** anthologies, he also syndicates his column from the **Montecito, California Journal** on the Senior Wire News Network. Best-selling side-splitter Christopher Moore has called Ernie "the Dave Barry of the West." In addition to his on-going, award-winning humor workshops, Ernie is a photographer, graduate of Brooks Institute. Admirers of Ernie's fine wit will want to check out his page at **www.erniesworld.com** and his books, *"Ernie's World"* and *"A Day In The Life of a 'Working' Writer*."

David Woodside is a freelance writer, a real estate entrepreneur and a former aerospace engineer (yes, he really was a rocket scientist). He has a book-in-progress of original palindrome creations. *REVERsed English: A Panoply Of Palindromes, Backward Bons Mots, Reversible Verses, And Other Adroit Drollery*. Lacking only a publisher, some illustrations and most of the chapters, this work is expected to be a valuable, time-saving book because you only have to read the first half. Woodside has contributed to journals and other periodicals and books, and he has won awards for his poetry, humor essays, and even a national competition for his complete short story of 75 one-syllable words. A long-time musician, he can be found writing songs, picking a mandolin and practicing a guitar in his underwear. How a guitar got in his underwear he doesn't know.

Love Good Humor?

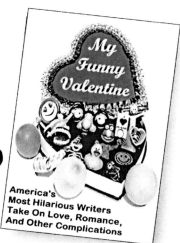

My Funny Valentine

America's Most Hilarious Writers Take On Love, Romance, And Other Complications

Then You'd Like Our Book of Love Humor

Some of the funniest writers alive turn their talents to romance, love, and how we deal with them on the designated day. A Vday stocking stuffer, nice gift for a lover, or just for laughs.

www.myfunnybooks.biz

adoro books.com

THANK YOU

For reading this book. We'd like to invite you to our mainstream imprint, Adoro Books, to see other books you might enjoy.

Our Two
Best-Selling
Humor Titles

www.adorobooks.com

BAUU
INSTITUTE
PRESS

Our publishing partner, Bauu Press,
a distinguished imprint for Native
American scholarship, also has some
very funny books you might like.

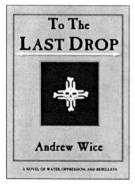

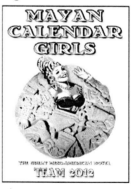

www.bauuinstitute.com

www.myfunnybooks.com

CPSIA information can be obtained at www.ICGtesting.com
Printed in the USA
BVOW010927081112

304980BV00007B/2/P

9 781936 955107